SIMONE BILES

ULTIMATE SPORTS HEROES

SIMONE BILES

GOING FOR GOLD

DINO

First published by Dino Books in 2021,
an imprint of Bonnier Books UK,
The Plaza, 535 King's Road, London SW10 0SZ
Owned by Bonnier Books,
Sveavägen 56, Stockholm, Sweden

@dinobooks
www.bonnierbooks.co.uk

Written by Charlotte Browne
Cover illustration by Bruce Huang

Paperback ISBN: 9781789463026
E-book ISBN: 9781789464351

British Library cataloguing-in-publication data:
A catalogue record for this book is available from the British Library.

Printed and bound in Great Britain by Clays Lltd, Elcograf S.p.A.

1 3 5 7 9 10 8 6 4 2

TABLE OF CONTENTS

CHAPTER 1

TINY BUT STRONG

'Hello, children. I'm Miss Doris and this is Mr Leo.'

Simone stared up at their warm, welcoming faces, then looked around wide-eyed and took in her new surroundings. The big, comfortable kitchen. Cookies on the table. And the small Beagle dog running between everyone's legs.

'And you must be Simone?' Miss Doris said, smiling at her. 'We're so pleased to see you and your sisters!'

Sitting next to Simone was her older sister, Ashley, holding their baby sister Adria in her arms. There had been so much change, but as

long as she, Ashley and Adria were together, Simone always felt safe.

'How old are you, Simone?' asked Miss Doris.

Simone gazed back at her, a bit overwhelmed. Then she felt a gentle squeeze on her fingers from Ashley and mustered the courage to speak.

'Three,' she murmured.

'She's not usually this shy,' Ashley explained to Miss Doris. 'It's... it's... a lot to take in. For all of us.'

The grown-ups smiled. They understood. Simone Biles and her siblings had travelled with their social worker, from Columbus, Ohio, where they had been living with their mum, who had been struggling to take care of them. Right now, the Biles children needed safety and support, and Miss Doris and Mr Leo were here to give it to them.

'We want you to feel at home here,' Mr Leo told them. 'Whatever you need, just ask us.'

'But first of all,' added Miss Doris, 'how about

some cookies and milkshakes?'

Ashley grinned. 'Yes, please!'

But Simone had glimpsed something even more exciting than cookies. Out of the window, she could see a huge yard where children were playing in the sun. She spotted a swing and, even more exciting... a trampoline!

As she turned to Miss Doris, her eyes were sparkling and a huge smile lit up her face. 'Can I play on it?'

Miss Doris shook her head. 'When you're a bit bigger, Simone. For now, it's just for the older kids.' She saw Simone's face fall and added, 'We wouldn't want you to get hurt, would we?'

'But...' Simone began, but Ashley gave her a warning look. Rules were rules, she knew that – even if she didn't like them.

'You'll soon be big enough,' Mr Leo told her. 'In the meantime, how about playing on the swing?'

A small smile returned to Simone's face. She loved the swings and the feeling of flying up into the air.

She had never had one in her own backyard before. Simone loved to be outside. It was where she was most fearless and her energy was boundless. She loved to run and jump, do handstands, cartwheels and roly-polys – it didn't matter where she was. Maybe there would be trees to climb too?

Wait, if Miss Doris and Mr Leo wouldn't let her bounce on the trampoline, they definitely wouldn't like her climbing trees.

Well, she just needed to show them how brave she was! Simone felt as safe scrambling around in the branches of a tree as she did on the ground. Why did grown-ups worry so much?

Simone and her sisters spent the rest of the day playing and exploring their new home. There was plenty of space to run about and the neighbourhood kids seemed friendly. Miss Doris and Mr Leo were kind, and there were drinks and snacks whenever they wanted them. Gradually the Biles children began to relax.

But when bedtime came, Simone felt a pang of

homesickness. It felt odd to be in a strange bed in a strange room, far from home. Miss Doris and Mr Leo had given the girls a room to themselves, and Simone was glad that her sisters were near. With her siblings beside her, she felt brave and strong.

'Can I sleep here?' she whispered, creeping over to Ashley's bed. 'Please?'

'You okay?' Ashley reached out and pulled her little sister into a hug. 'It's been a big day.'

Simone nodded. All the new things she had seen and done whirled around her head. Miss Doris and Mr Leo. A different house. Different food. New kids. New games. And tomorrow? More new things. More changes.

Ashley lifted up the duvet. 'Snuggle in,' she said. 'It'll be okay. I'll always look after you.'

Simone climbed in beside Ashley and curled up close to her and, within minutes, she was asleep and dreaming.

The Biles children settled quickly into their new home. They loved the freedom Miss Doris and Mr

Leo gave them to play outside as much as they liked, and the grown-ups quickly spotted Simone's athletic ability. At just three years old, the little girl seemed to have never-ending energy. She was quick and agile, running around the yard all day, playing games and chasing the dog.

'You've got lightning legs, Simone,' laughed Miss Doris.

'Yeah. That mutt doesn't stand a chance!' grinned Mr Leo.

But, despite their encouragement, to Simone's despair she still wasn't allowed to play on the trampoline!

Instead, Simone took out her energy on the swing. Kicking her legs furiously, she swung herself up, up, up, squealing with delight as gravity brought her whooshing back down. The higher she went, the more she whooped. High enough to peer over the wall. High enough to give her stomach a funny somersault feeling. High enough to make Miss Doris and Mr Leo shout out in alarm.

'Not so high, Simone!'

Gripping the chains of the swing with both hands, she swung higher and higher, her braids flying out behind her. And when she saw one of the other kids do a backflip, leaping off the swing and landing on two feet, she knew she had to try it too.

Here goes!

Propelling herself as high as she could, she let go of the chain and flung her body off the seat and launched into the backflip. 'Wheeeeeeee!' Simone squealed with delight as she flew through the air. 'Whoooooeeeeeeee!'

She landed on the grass with a thud. Miss Doris, who had been watching with alarm from the kitchen window, rushed out of the back door. Was little Simone hurt?

But despite a bit of a bruising, Simone was happy and giggling, delighted that she'd managed a proper backflip 'Again, again!' she cried. 'I want to do it again!'

Ashley ran over. 'Wow! Simone! That was amazing!'

But Miss Doris was concerned. 'Please don't encourage her!' She told Ashley, sighing. Then she bent over Simone. 'You must be careful. You could have hurt yourself!'

'But I didn't, not really!' Simone leapt up as if her feet were on springs.

'Well, well. You are a force of nature.' Miss Doris shook her head in astonishment. Her mind flew back to earlier that morning when she had caught Simone sitting on the kitchen counter trying to pry open the cookie jar. The top of the counter was double Simone's height!

'Simone! How did you get up there?!' she had asked.

'I jumped.'

Miss Doris was so surprised she took a moment to tell Simone off for trying to take a cookie without asking. 'Next time, please just ask. I'd hate you to hurt yourself! Promise me?'

Simone nodded gravely and Miss Doris handed her a cookie.

But the days of leaping around in Miss Doris and Mr Leo's kitchen and flying through the air on the swing were soon to come to an end. One morning, Simone was playing in the living room with baby Adria when Ashley rushed in.

'Grandpa Ron is here!' she whispered.

A tall man with a salt and pepper goatee beard entered the room. In a warm Texan drawl, he greeted each of the children in turn, giving them a big, beaming smile.

'Hi, Grandpa,' said Ashley.

'Hi, Hampaw', said Simone. At three, she still couldn't pronounce her g's properly.

Grandpa laughed. 'Hampaw! I like that!'

When he laughed, Simone felt warm inside. She was too young to remember seeing her grandparents as a baby, but already Grandpa Ron felt like family.

'Where's Grandma Nellie?' asked Ashley.

'Well, she's back home in Texas. She's really

looking forward to seeing you all.'

The children looked at each other.

'Are we having a holiday?' asked Ashley.

Their grandpa smiled. 'Yes, think of it as a holiday – with us.'

'Is Mum still getting better?' asked Ashley, her face full of concern.

Grandpa nodded. 'Your mum's doing well. She's thinking of you.'

'So we're going to Texas?'

'Houston, Texas,' Grandpa replied. 'A place called Spring just outside, to be exact. Remember, that's where Grandma and I live. And you know what else there is in Texas?' he added.

'What?' Ashley and little Simone were all ears.

'The best pecan pie and barbecued ribs in the world.'

Well, Simone definitely liked the sound of that.

So the children said goodbye to Miss Doris and Mr Leo, and drove with their grandpa to the airport. Simone had never been on a plane before.

'It's a three-hour flight,' he told them. 'Think you can keep still for three hours?'

Ashley laughed. 'Simone can't keep still for three minutes!'

Grandpa smiled. 'Twitchy feet, eh, Simone?'

Simone nodded. Her energy was bubbling up inside. She longed to spring out of her seat and run up and down the aisle, then clamber up over the seats and swing from the overhead lockers. But Grandpa had buckled her seatbelt tight.

'You have to wear this while we take off,' he told her. 'Everyone does. Otherwise the pilot won't fly the plane.'

So Simone sat as still as she could. Soon they were motoring down the runway, gathering speed until – whoosh! The plane left the ground and soared up into the air. There was a funny, flippy feeling in Simone's stomach, a bit like when she had swung really high on the swing.

'Exciting, isn't it?' grinned Grandpa. 'We're on an adventure.'

During the journey, Grandpa told Simone about when she had been a baby. It was because of Grandpa that she was called Simone.

'I'm a fan of Nina Simone. Have you heard of her?' He smiled as Simone shook her head. 'She's a very famous singer. So I suggested to your mum that she call you Simone, and she did.'

That made Simone smile. 'I'll play you some of her music when we get home,' added Grandpa. 'Do you like music?'

Simone nodded. She loved music. Particularly dancing to it.

Listening to her grandpa talk, Simone managed to sit still for a whole three hours.

Finally, they reached Houston airport and were bundled off the plane with the other passengers. From across the crowded arrivals hall, Simone spotted a short woman with curly hair waving at them.

'Look, it's Grandma,' said Ashley.

'Hamma!' said Simone.

Grandpa laughed again. 'Hamma, I think she'll like that.'

Grandma had hugs for all of the children, including baby Adria. She had kind eyes, just like Grandpa, and Simone felt safe in an instant. It felt like she had known Grandma all her life.

'Welcome, everyone, it's so good to see you.' Grandma led the way to the car. 'Spring is just north of Houston. We'll be there in 25 minutes.'

When they reached Spring and Grandpa and Grandma's home, Simone leapt out of the car. She was fizzing with energy and excitement.

'Welcome to your new home,' Grandma told them with a smile. 'Girls, let me show you your room.'

Simone ran on ahead up the stairs. She couldn't wait to see it.

'Wow – you're a bundle of energy aren't you, Miss Simone!' Grandma laughed, holding open the door for them.

Simone's eyes were wide with delight. 'Ashley – look! A bunk bed!'

Grandma turned to Ashley. 'Are you happy to sleep on the top? You're the oldest.'

Ashley smiled. 'Well yeah, sure, that's if Simone doesn't break it first. She's so energetic!'

Simone was already swinging from the wooden slats underneath the top bunk. 'Weeeeee!'

'Oh, Simone! Do be careful!' Grandma cried in alarm.

Simone somersaulted from the bed to the floor.

'Girls, I have some Barbie dolls here for you. Why don't you play with these instead?' said Grandma.

Ashley's face lit up, but Simone wasn't looking at the dolls. Outside, she had spotted something far more exciting. She ran over to the window and climbed onto a chair to get a better look. Could it be? It seemed too good to be true!

Down in the yard, another trampoline...

Excitement began to bubble inside her. But – wait. Maybe Grandma, like Miss Doris and Mr Leo, would think she was too little to play on it. Simone held her breath. *Please, Hamma! Please!*

she thought.

Her grandma smiled at her. 'Ah... the trampoline! I thought you might like it. Would you like to play on it now?'

Simone couldn't believe her luck. 'Really?'

'Yes, of course, honey, you could do with working off some energy before dinner time!'

Grandma and Ashley exchanged a grin as they watched Simone bound down the stairs and out into the yard. She flung herself onto the trampoline and – whoosh! She was away, bouncing and tumbling, whooping with delight, soaring higher and higher.

'Well, we have a right little bundle of energy on our hands here,' said Grandma. 'Does she always have this much energy?'

Ashley nodded. 'Always!' she grinned.

Hours passed as Simone flipped and twisted on the trampoline, lost in her own little world. Suddenly, she heard her grandma's voice, calling her in for dinner.

CHAPTER 2

HOME FOR GOOD

As the weeks went by, Simone's happiness grew and grew. Running around in the yard, bouncing on the trampoline, playing games with Ashley, she had never felt more at home. Grandma and Grandpa were kind and easy-going. It was only at mealtimes when the smile fell from Simone's face and frustration came pouring out. Dinner combined her two least favourite things: sitting still and having to eat meat and vegetables!

'Simone, you know the drill, you can't get up from the table until you've finished.'

'I don't like it, Hamma, the meat's too chewy...

and the vegetables... ugh.'

'They're part of a healthy diet, Simone. You can't eat pasta and pizza all the time.'

Simone would *definitely* eat pasta and pizza all the time if she could!

But she had found a trick. When no one was looking, she took the horrible meat and veg and stuck it in a hole underneath her seat. All gone!

She couldn't fool Grandma for long, though. 'Oh, Simone! It's such a waste of food!'

Simone felt a sudden pang of guilt. 'Sorry, Hamma.' She hated it when Grandma looked disappointed.

'You are a stubborn thing sometimes, Simone.' Grandma shook her head and sighed. 'I have an idea. How about I mush up your meat and give it to you with noodles?'

Simone looked at her with a smile. Mushed up? That could work. 'Ok, Hamma.'

'Shake on it?' suggested Grandma.

Simone nodded. They smiled at each other and

shook hands.

'You're a force to be reckoned with, Simone Biles!'

The months flew by and with each day, Simone felt happier and more settled, as if they had always lived here. In fact, sometimes she found it hard to remember her life before Grandma and Grandpa.

Then one day, Simone's mother came to visit. Grandma and Grandpa had told the children a few days earlier, but somehow it hadn't seemed real to Simone. When her mother walked in the door, Simone hung back, feeling suddenly shy and uneasy. It seemed so long ago that they had lived together. Ashley flew into her arms, but Simone clung onto her Grandma's hand, feelings of confusion whirling in her head.

'Your mother wants you to all live as a family again,' Grandpa told them that evening when their mother had gone.

Ashley squealed with excitement, but Simone

didn't share her joy. She was so happy here with her grandparents. She didn't want to leave. The thought of more change made her feel sad and anxious. She would miss them as much as her older sister missed their mother.

In the end, the family's social worker found a solution that suited everyone. Ashley would live with foster parents in Cleveland, to be close to her mother's home in Columbus. Simone and baby Adria would stay in Texas with their grandparents. Simone felt sad saying goodbye to her sister; they had never been apart like this before. But the feeling of joy at living permanently with Grandma and Grandpa was overwhelming.

Best of all, Simone and Adria would be in Houston to celebrate Christmas. Grandma and Grandpa's house was alight with sparkling decorations and the smell of turkey and pumpkin pie wafted from the kitchen. Simone felt as though she'd wandered into her own Christmas miracle. She hugged her grandma tight.

'Is this really forever, Grandma?' she asked. Simone could now pronounce her g's.

'You bet, sweetheart.' Grandma held her close and Simone could see tears in her eyes.

One evening, after Christmas, Simone's grandparents called Simone and Adria down from their rooms. The look on their faces was serious and excited at the same time.

'We have some news, girls. Today, we officially adopted you.'

Simone stared back at them with wide eyes. Adopted?

'It means we are now your legal parents,' Grandpa Ron explained.

'So you can call me Mom now, and Grandpa, Dad. If you want to, of course,' said Grandma Nellie. 'We don't mind what you call us.'

Simone flung herself into her grandma's arms and Adria followed. Grandpa folded his arms around the three of them and there they stayed. Simone's feeling of joy was overwhelming.

That evening, as she brushed her teeth, Simone let Nellie's words float around in her mind. Mom. Dad. Gradually they began to sink in, and suddenly she found herself flying down the stairs and flinging open the kitchen door, bursting to say the words out loud.

'Mom?'

Nellie looked up. 'Yes, Simone?'

Simone turned to Ron.

'Dad?'

'How can I help, honey?'

A huge smile spread over Simone's face. 'Nothing!' she called as she ran back out of the room as fast as she had come.

Her new parents looked at each other and smiled. Simone's joy was infectious. In fact, they could barely imagine what it had been like before this little hurricane of energy had come into their lives. How proud they were to be the parents of this bright, mischievous, energetic girl!

CHAPTER 3

TIME TO TUMBLE

It was summer of 2003 and Simone had turned six. She was getting more energetic with every year that passed. Sit still? She simply couldn't! Not when there were yards to run in, trees to climb and parks to play in. Everyone who knew her – friends, family, teachers – noticed her boundless energy, as well as her sunny personality.

Simone's favourite thing to do was performing tricks on the trampoline. Her teenage 'brothers', Adam and Ron Junior – her grandparents' sons – marvelled at how high she could fly and how many flips she could do before landing on her feet – far more than they could. And if she wasn't springing around on the trampoline, she was using her brothers as climbing frames, clambering up on to their shoulders and swinging from their outstretched arms. Sometimes her mom would come running out to the yard in alarm.

'Boys! Remember, she's still so little. Be careful!'

But Simone was never scared of hurting herself, especially with Adam and Ron there to catch her.

'It's us you should be worried about, Mom,' laughed Adam. 'She'll break us one of these days!'

And it wasn't just at home where Simone's energy was limitless. At the daycare centre she attended, it was all her teachers could do to make her stay in one place for 10 minutes to eat her lunch. Her heart would sink when the teachers announced an activity that involved sitting still. While the other kids loved puzzles and colouring in, Simone was desperate to be running around, swinging from the monkey bars or impressing her friends with handstands and backflips.

Today, though, Simone's teachers had something else in store. Adam, who volunteered at the daycare centre along with Ron Junior, broke the news.

'We're going to visit a farm!' he announced to Simone and the other children.

A farm? The children began to chatter excitedly. Would they get to ride a tractor? And feed the animals? Would there be a quiz? And outdoor games? Simone was already fizzing with excitement.

'Okay, everyone, let's get changed into our field-trip uniform,' Ron Junior told them. He handed out brightly-coloured T-shirts and the children pulled them on over their clothes. 'We want to be able to spot you easily.'

But within a few minutes, rain was hammering against the windowpanes. Simone groaned. She knew this would spoil their plans. The teachers never took them outside when it was pouring down. She wondered what they would decide to do instead.

Please don't send us to a museum, she thought to

herself. *Please don't make us do more colouring in.* She watched anxiously as Adam, Ron Junior and the other teachers gathered together.

Finally, Adam spoke to the class. 'Okay, guys, change of plan. We're going to a tumbling gym instead. Who has heard of Bannon's Gymnastix?'

Simone had never heard of Bannon's. But the word 'tumble' made her spirits lift immediately.

'I think you're going to have fun there, Simone,' Adam told her. 'Without the danger of injuring yourself – or me!'

Sure enough, as Simone entered Bannon's Gymnastix her eyes lit up. As far as she could see, there were kids, teenagers and grown-ups tumbling, flipping, balancing and swinging on weird and wonderful equipment.

Adam grinned, seeing the delight on his little sister's face. 'Thought you'd like it!'

'Wow!' she breathed. 'Can I try it all?'

'Of course! That's why we're here.'

The class gathered round as one of the staff

explained about the different equipment and how to use it. Simone's head whirled as she took in the strange names: low beams, low bars, uneven bars, floor vaults, springboards, foam pits. It looked like so much fun! Her eyes were immediately drawn to the older gymnasts, dressed in leotards.

'Why are their hands covered in dust?' she asked.

'It's chalk. It stops their hands slipping,' the instructor explained.

Simone watched as a girl balanced on the low bar before bending backwards and flipping onto her hands.

I want to do that, thought Simone.

The next hour was pretty much the best fun Simone had ever had. She moved from one piece of apparatus to the next, flipping and swinging, copying moves she saw the older gymnasts perform: from a front handspring on the vault to a cartwheel on the mat and a front tuck on the beam mat. As soon as she had performed a trick on one piece of equipment, there was something new to try. And as she flung herself into increasingly acrobatic twists and turns, her whole body quivered with excitement. She couldn't believe it was possible to have so much fun in one place!

'Are you up for a challenge, Simone?' Adam called her over. 'How about a backflip into the foam pit?'

'You bet!'

Grinning from ear to ear, Simone threw herself into a neat backflip. Without thinking, she added a twist before landing in the heap of foam bricks at the bottom of the pit.

'Well done!' Adam applauded.

Simone crawled her way out of the foam pit. Already she had an idea for how to make her backflip better and more impressive.

'Adam! Watch this!'

But when she turned to look at her brother, he was busy talking to someone: a woman, whose gaze seemed to be locked on Simone.

Adam called her over. 'Simone, this lady is

called Ronnie. She's a coach here and she'd like to speak to you.'

'Are you enjoying yourself, Simone?' asked Ronnie, and Simone nodded. 'You've got good, what we call, "air awareness",' she continued.

Simone grinned. She didn't know what that meant but it sounded like a compliment. 'Thank you.'

'Try a cartwheel for me, Simone. But rather than keeping your feet separate when you land, bring them together and land on both of them.'

Simone followed Ronnie's instructions, turning a neat cartwheel before landing with her feet together.

'Bravo! You've just performed a "round-off",' Ronnie told her. 'It's a popular move with cheerleaders. You can keep building on that by adding a back handspring or a back tuck.'

Round-off? Back tuck? Simone looked confused.

'Have you done any gymnastics before, Simone?'

'No – never,' she replied.

'Would you like to try some classes?'

Simone's face lit up. 'Yes – I'd love to!'

'Well, we'll have to check with Mom and Dad,' said Adam. But his smile told her he would do everything he could to persuade them.

That afternoon, Simone handed Ronnie's letter to her mother. It invited her to take gymnastics classes at the gym. Simone had promise, the letter said. She had raw talent.

'It was so much fun,' said Simone. 'Can I go? Please, Mom, please!'

'We'll see,' said her mother. 'I'm not making any promises. I'll have to speak to your father. It's a big commitment.'

Simone clenched her fingers into nervous fists. What if he said no? She hoped with all her heart that he would agree!

Later that night, after dinner, Nellie and Ron discussed the gymnastics proposal.

'I think we should let her go,' said Nellie. 'She was over the moon when she came back. She clearly loved it.'

Simone's father smiled. 'She spends all day jumping and climbing. This could be an outlet for all her energy.'

They looked at each other and grinned. They knew how delighted their daughter would be.

'Simone, honey, come in here for a minute!' called Dad. 'These gymnastics classes, you really want to do them, don't you?'

Simone nodded enthusiastically.

'Well, we agree that it's a great idea. You can start later this week.'

Simone's heart leapt. Yes! Her mom and dad were the best! 'Thank you!' she yelled. 'Thank you so much!'

So Nellie enrolled Simone and Adria in twice-weekly gymnastics classes. To Simone's delight, her coach was Ronnie, who'd encouraged her on her first visit to Bannon's. And it seemed all the hours she had spent bouncing on the trampoline at home had paid off.

'You've got great power, air balance and energy,' Ronnie told her. 'Now we need to work on your form and technique.'

Ronnie showed Simone the correct way to perform the flips and somersaults and twists that she had been practising on her trampoline at home, and she gave her strengthening exercises to build up her muscles. 'These will help when we go on to more complex moves,' Ronnie told her. And there were 'drills' too: small sections of a skill that were broken down and worked on separately, then put together into a final sequence.

One of the first skills that Ronnie taught Simone was the 'kip': a simple but challenging movement that a gymnast uses to lift themselves up onto a piece of equipment called the 'uneven bars'. It required strong arms and legs, but Simone had both, and Ronnie was impressed by how quickly she picked up the skill.

'Keep your arms straight and your feet stretched out in front of the bar,' Ronnie called. 'And kick up a bit more strongly.'

Simone mastered this quickly, kicking with control and swinging up onto the bar.

'Well done!' said Ronnie, as Simone landed smoothly back on the floor. 'Now, I'd like you to do it again to show Aimee.' She smiled at the older girl next to her. 'Aimee, watch Simone carefully.'

Simone knew that Aimee was both Ronnie's daughter and a coach at Bannon's too, and she really wanted to impress Aimee and make Ronnie proud. She performed the kip again while they watched. Her movements were stronger and more precise each time.

'You can't deny, we have a natural here,' Ronnie said to Aimee.

Aimee nodded. 'That was impressive,' she said. 'How old are you, Simone?'

'Six.' Simone smiled up at her.

'She's incredibly powerful for a six-year-old,' Aimee said to Ronnie. She turned to Simone. 'I think we can expect great things from you, Simone.

You enjoy working hard, don't you?'

Simone nodded. She did!

'Well, keep up the good work!' Aimee grinned at her before returning to her class. There was no doubt in her mind. Little Simone Biles had something very special.

As well as giving her an outlet for her energy, gymnastics also gave Simone another opportunity: to wear the sparkly, colourful leotards that Nellie had bought her. Tumbling about wearing her favourite pink and purple outfits, somehow her confidence was even higher. She felt like a proper gymnast already!

With her technical skills improving session by session, it wasn't long before Simone moved into Bannon's USAG (which stands for United States of America Gymnastics) Junior Olympic Programme. If she wanted to compete in state, regional and eventually national competitions, Simone would have to make her way through the 10 different levels set by USAG, and every gymnast had to perform the same routine to showcase the skills they'd mastered. Simone was excited. She loved to perform in front of her coaches and couldn't wait for the opportunity to show what she could do in front of a larger audience.

Her first opportunity was at a recital held by Bannon's. It was just a few weeks after Simone had joined the programme and she couldn't wait to show her parents what she could do.

'Do you feel nervous?' Ronnie asked her as she prepared for her first exercise.

Simone shook her head. A huge smile spread across her face. 'Just excited!' she replied.

The first exercise involved climbing 10 feet up a rope using only her arms, with her legs stretched out in front of her. To the astonishment of Nellie, Ron and the rest of the audience, Simone reached the top of the rope in seconds – and then carried on climbing! In just a few seconds, her powerful little arms had taken her 20 feet up in the air.

Nellie's heart skipped a beat as she watched her

small daughter dangling from the ceiling so high up – and it wasn't long before Ronnie stepped in to coax her down.

'Well done, Simone, but can you come down now please? You're pretty high up there!'

To the relief of the audience, Simone scrambled down as easily as she had gone up.

Next up was the vault, a sort of table with sloping sides and a springy top, over a metre high. Simone watched as the children ahead of her in the line-up sprinted down the runway and launched themselves off the small springboard onto the vault itself, landing upside down on their hands, before tumbling off the other side of the vault to land on the mat. It was a simple move – and Simone knew she could beat the others!

She felt the power building up in her muscles as she flew down the runway. *Here goes!* She bounced firmly on the springboard, then soared through the air, her hands barely brushing the vault. Up, up, up she went, landing at the other end of the mat with her feet neatly together and a huge smile on her face.

Ronnie and Aimee were staring at her in disbelief. Then she heard Ronnie say: 'Now, that's what I call a vault!'

In the audience, Nellie and Ron were beaming with pride. Simone was shaping up to be quite a gymnast! The decision to let her take classes had definitely been the right one!

Over the next few months, Simone progressed so well through the Junior Olympic Programme levels that it wasn't long before she'd reached level five.

Ronnie had given Simone a long list of skills she had to work on: long-hang pullovers on the bar, split jumps on the beam, straddle jumps and round off back handspring back tucks on the floor.

'There are so many moves!' she said to Ronnie.

'Yes, but you can already do all these moves,' said Ronnie. 'These are the basics that every gymnast builds on before learning more complex moves. Now you need to work on your finishing details.'

Simone sighed. Finishing details were vital, but they were the part she enjoyed least: making sure her toes were pointed, her knees were pressed together and her arms were fully extended. But it wasn't enough to perform with strength and speed. Simone knew her performances had to be as polished as possible.

'We need to work on your stick too,' said Ronnie.

Simone frowned. 'Stick?'

'Yes, you should always aim to "stick" your landing. If you can land straight on your feet without hopping, that's a perfect stick.'

'I do hop a lot when I land,' Simone admitted.

'Don't worry, it's early days,' Ronnie reassured her. 'You have amazing raw ability, Simone. Your balance in the air is incredible. There is plenty of time to perfect the details.'

Simone smiled. It was true. She always felt as though she knew where she was as she flipped and twisted her way through the air. It was like she had an inner compass. Other gymnasts often count in their heads to keep track of where they are, but Simone never got lost. She always launched and flipped and landed with perfect timing.

She also had a fearless attitude. One day, she spotted a cheerleader perform a standing 'back tuck': a backflip with legs tucked into the chest.

'I can do that!' she told Aimee and Ronnie.

'Hmm, I'm not sure about that, Simone,' Aimee said, doubtfully. 'It took me several sessions to master a back tuck when I was learning.'

Simone stood on the mat and, without hesitation, jumped up into the air, flipping over her own shoulders, her hips skyward and her legs pulled tightly into her chest.

'Wow.' Aimee was impressed. 'Ok, Simone, let's see if you can do it on the beam?'

'Sure!' Simone darted straight to the high beam.

The coaches ran after her. 'Wait! Not the high beam! The floor beam! Simone – stop!'

But it was too late. Simone was sailing through the air. Ronnie and Aimee stared at each other in surprise. Was there no limit to what this girl could do?

After the class, Aimee went over to speak to Nellie. 'I think Simone has something special,' she told her. 'I know she's still only seven but if she's prepared to work hard, I think she could make it to the Nationals, the Worlds, maybe even the Olympics.'

Nellie blinked in surprise. She knew Simone was talented – but the Olympics? It was amazing to think that her girl had such potential.

And as for working hard... 'No one works harder than Simone,' smiled Nellie. 'There are definitely no worries there!'

CHAPTER 4

STICKING POWER

'If you can master the "giant", you'll have a foundation for much harder moves on the bar and more difficult dismounts.'

Simone frowned. Out of all four bits of apparatus – the floor, the vault, the balance beam and the uneven bars – the uneven bars were her least favourite. She was still little for her age and struggled with the grip she needed because of her small hands. The giant involved swinging through 360 degrees with straight legs. For the first time, Simone faced a real challenge.

Ronnie was there to help her. She held Simone's

lower back and kept one hand on her arm to keep her steady. With her coach's help, she swung round in a full circle, her legs straight and her back slightly arched. 'I think you've got it!' said Ronnie. 'That's much better.'

'Can I try on my own now?' asked Simone.

'Okay, give it a go on the high bar.'

Simone bounced over to the high bar and swung herself into the air, completing two rotations on her own. But as she wheeled into her next rotation, her hands slipped from the bar and she crashed down to the floor, crying out in pain as she missed the protective foam mat.

Fear was not an emotion Simone felt very often. But as she lay staring up at the ceiling, tears began welling up in her eyes. Suddenly, the thought of swinging over the bar again terrified her. Maybe she wasn't as strong as she thought?

Ronnie rushed over. 'Are you alright, Simone?' She put out a hand to pull Simone to her feet. 'Up you get and have another go.'

'I don't want to do that again! Please don't make me.'

'Come on. You can do this,' Ronnie said encouragingly. 'Don't let the fear get in your head.'

'No!' Simone protested, feeling the tears well up again. 'I can't.'

'By the time we finish today, you'll be doing giants. I promise you.'

But Simone had other ideas. She stood defiantly, with her hands on her hips.

Ronnie looked her in the eyes. 'You're used to finding things easy, Simone. But there is an important lesson here. Don't give up on a bad day. You can do this.'

Simone grimaced. But she gritted her teeth and allowed Ronnie to lift her back onto the high bar. Then, with Ronnie's hand supporting her, she managed to spin round the bar, once, twice, three times...

But as soon as Ronnie stepped back, leaving her to spin on her own, Simone started to panic.

'I'm not going to make it!' she yelped.

'Keep calm, Simone. You can do this. Imagine your body is a spoke in a wheel – fully stretch your legs and point your toes.'

With every muscle clenched, Simone raised herself to the top of the bar. Her heart was pounding as she began to swing round in a big circle. Would she? Could she?

'That's it!' Ronnie clapped her hands together. 'Well done, Simone!'

Simone could hardly believe it. The 'giant' had taken her outside her comfort zone. But she had done it. She had managed to overcome her fear and had mastered this tricky skill.

As Ronnie helped her down from the bar, Simone breathed a sigh of relief. That was enough for today!

It wasn't long before Simone's coaches agreed that she was ready to move up to level seven. Here she would have the opportunity to develop her own routines and perform them at larger state and regional events. Ronnie and Aimee were excited.

Simone's potential was endless, they believed.

But before she could progress to the next level, Simone had to take a test, which involved performing all the complex skills she'd learned so far. Ronnie and Aimee agreed that Simone was the most talented youngster they had seen at Bannon's for many years. Possibly ever. They expected her to pass with flying colours.

So it was a huge surprise to everyone – including Simone – when she failed.

By now, Aimee had taken over Simone's coaching. She could see how disappointed Simone was and took her aside. 'Is something wrong?' she asked. 'I've never seen you fall off so many beams! And your tumbling passes? You didn't stick any of your landings.'

Simone looked at her feet. 'I don't think I know the skills well enough.'

Aimee smiled kindly. 'Okay, thanks for being honest with me. That's something we can work on. But it does mean putting in lots of practice!'

Simone nodded eagerly. She would do whatever it took! So she worked with Aimee till she knew her routine inside and out. By the time she took the test again, her twists and tumbles, spins and somersaults were perfect. She was able to enjoy the feeling of soaring through the air. It all felt fun again.

'Yes – I knew you could do it!' Aimee high-fived her. 'But, we have more work to do on bars.'

Simone groaned.

'You fall into a category of gymnast that we describe as "power gymnasts," explained Aimee. 'So you're going to find bars harder.'

Simone looked puzzled. Power gymnast? 'What does that mean?'

'Power gymnasts tend to be better at controlling the apparatus. You have so much strength in your muscles, you can flip and twist to your heart's content. But with the bar, you have to give up some control and let it swing you around.'

Simone was proud of her strong muscles. But it

seemed they were more of a problem when it came to uneven bars and she still wasn't confident. She made up her mind to speak to Aimee.

'Can I just specialise in beam, vault and floor?' asked Simone.

Aimee smiled. 'Don't let this fear of the bar block you, Simone. You have the makings of an excellent all-around gymnast. But you'll need to get your teeth stuck into all four events. Think of it as a challenge.'

'Okay...' Simone smiled, bravely. She was always up for a challenge, and she was determined to work even harder. As much as she hated the uneven bars, she hated the thought of not competing as an all-around gymnast even more. She spent as much time as she could training on the bars, repeating the same skills until she got the hang of them.

'I can see how hard you're working,' Aimee told her, impressed. She knew that focusing on one exercise over and over was more of a challenge for Simone than it was for many other children because

Simone had recently been diagnosed with ADHD, or Attention Deficit Hyperactivity Disorder. This meant that Simone found it hard to sit still or do the same activity for long periods of time, both in and out of the gym. She got bored easily and preferred to move on, testing herself in new ways. But ADHD was also her superpower. It allowed her to think fast and throw herself into new challenges with great energy.

One of the trickiest moves for Simone to master on the uneven bars was the 'straddle back'. Here she had to swing backwards with her legs straddled before letting go of the high bar to swoop through the air and catch the low bar and spin around it.

But with her dedication and determination, Simone mastered the straddle back within a few months, and was already training for level 10 skills. At just 10 years old, Simone was the only gymnast at Bannon's who'd got that far. She was on the verge of becoming an elite level gymnast. Other gymnasts would stop by to gawp at her practice sessions, awed by her skills. And at regional competitions, she was already wowing the judges. Simone's performances were magnetic!

'We're so impressed with how far you've come. But this is where you and I start learning together,' Aimee told her one day.

'Really?'

'Yeah, I would have loved to compete beyond level eight but I broke my leg at the age of 14 and I had to stop.'

Simone's face fell. 'Oh Aimee, I'm sorry.'

Aimee winked at her. 'You'll just have to fulfil my dreams for me. No pressure.'

Simone grinned. 'You got it.'

'It will take extra work though, Simone, if you want to go elite. It will take hours of training after school. It's not going to be easy.'

But in the few years she'd been training at Bannon's, Simone had fallen head over heels for gymnastics and she'd faced every challenge with courage and hard work. It had more than paid off, and she was happy to carry on putting in the extra work!

At the South Padre international meet in 2008, at the age of just 11, Simone Biles won the all-around highest score.

Some of the coaches at Bannon's were concerned Simone might achieve too much too soon, and drop out from exhaustion or injury. But Aimee knew what Simone was capable of and how strong and focused she was, and she didn't want to hold her back.

Simone didn't want to be held back either. She was already thinking ahead to the 2012 Olympics in four years' time, and the prospect of getting a place on the national team. The only problem was, she would still only be 15. To compete, she had to be 16. Would she really have to wait until the next Olympic Games in 2016? Eight whole years away? It felt like a lifetime!

That night she opened up her diary, which she'd started to write in regularly.

'I don't know if I will make it,' she wrote, doubts and uncertainty whirling round in her mind. She closed her diary and turned over to go to sleep. But sleep wouldn't come that night. She knew she had been blessed with a special talent. It was up to her to make the most of it. Only she could do that.

After a restless few hours she sat up and turned the light back on. Opening her diary, she started writing again.

'I want to go the furthest I can.'

As she stared at the words on the page, her hopes and dreams suddenly became clear. Yes, she would do everything it took to go the furthest she could.

And she hoped that might mean the US women's national team.

CHAPTER 5

A NEW ADDITION TO THE FAMILY

Simone's dad, Ron, looked at her across the table with a concerned expression on his face. 'What score do you need to get?'

'Thirty-four,' Simone replied.

It was April 2008, and Simone was about to compete in another regional meet: the Region 3 Championships. Thirty-four was the minimum score she needed to qualify for the level nine Western Championships, which would be held the following month.

There was a lot riding on these Championships. There would be officials from the USAG attending, as well as the famous gymnastics coach and talent scout, Márta Károlyi. Márta, or Martha as she was known, was in charge of choosing the national team and had trained world and Olympic champions. If she was impressed with Simone's performance, Simone might get an invite to train with her in Texas. There was no one in the sport who had more power to shape a gymnast's future than Martha did. Simone was desperate to impress her!

'Do you feel ready enough to take this on, Simone? You're putting yourself under a lot of pressure.'

'You know what would make me feel less stressed, Dad?' A mischievous grin spread across Simone's face. 'My very own puppy.'

'Simone! We're not getting a dog. End of. We've discussed this.'

'But look how well Adria and I look after Bo!' Bo was their neighbour's dog who they walked and fed when their neighbours went away.

Ron sighed. 'Okay, Simone, how about this... if you qualify for the Westerns, you can have a dog.'

Simone leapt up to give him a hug. 'Thank you, thank you, Dad! I won't let you down! I won't let myself down!'

Her dad groaned. 'What have we let ourselves in for?'

For the next few weeks, Simone practised her heart out. The competition scoring system for a routine was complicated, based on the level of difficulty of a skill (or 'D') and its execution (or 'E'). Each routine started with a base mark of 10 and points would be deducted for small, medium and large errors. Simone knew her routine would have to be pretty much perfect. But she had never been more motivated. As she swung and flipped and tumbled, along with endless practice drills, she visualised going to the nearby farm to pick out a puppy!

On the day of the Region 3 Championships, Simone bounced into the arena full of confidence. First up was floor exercise. The floor was her favourite event. It allowed her to show off her strength, flexibility and air balance – as well as express her personality. For 90 seconds, she revelled in the joy of somersaulting, cartwheeling and jumping through the air. She finished her routine to thunderous applause, along with whoops and cheers from her parents and Adria.

She excelled on the balance beam and the vault, and even felt confident on the uneven bars. She had worked hard to improve her power, speed and technique. As she performed the Cuervo – a front handspring with a half twist into a back tuck – she even found herself enjoying it!

But would her final score be enough to secure a place at the Western Championships?

Yes! Simone's heart soared as her final score appeared on the screen. 38.100, four points over the minimum she'd needed to achieve. She'd placed first on floor and second all-around. Her eyes flew to her family, watching from the stands. Eight-year-old Adria was squealing with delight. Her mom was grinning from ear to ear. And her dad? He looked a little more subdued. Simone knew why... He was thinking of the chaos a new puppy would bring!

But as he caught Simone's eye, her dad couldn't help smiling too. Puppy or no puppy, he was brimming with pride for his talented daughter.

It was a few months before the Bileses made the trip to a nearby farm to pick out their new dog. But finally the big day arrived, and Simone's heart melted as they walked from cage to cage looking at the puppies staring up at them.

'Oh I wish we could take them all!' she cried.

'This is not going to turn into 101 Dalmations!' her dad said firmly.

'Hey, what about this one?' Her mom pointed over to a black and brown puppy, a German Shepherd, who was skipping excitedly about the cage.

'She's got a lot of energy, hasn't she? She's a bit like you, Simone,' said Ron.

One of the handlers opened the cage and placed the puppy in Simone's arms. Her face lit up as the puppy snuggled into her, reaching up to lick her face.

'Yes – this one! She's adorable! Do you mind if I name her?' Simone asked her little sister.

'Sure,' replied Adria, 'you did win her after all.'

'How about Maggie Elena Biles?' suggested Simone.

Her sister grinned – and Maggie wagged her tiny tail in agreement.

***

As August came round there was also the excitement of the Beijing Olympics. Simone was glued to the TV as the gymnastics competition unfolded. The USA's Nastia Liukin was tipped for the gold, and Simone's heart was in her mouth as she watched Nastia take her run-up for the vault, which was her weakest skill. With a look of steely determination on her face, Nastia performed a perfect double twist in the air, with an equally perfect landing, to achieve a score of 15.025. She achieved even better scores on the uneven bars and beam at 16.650 and 16.125. In her final event on floor, she scored 15.525 to see off reigning World Champion, Shawn Johnson, and took gold in the individual all-around. Simone's cheers were ear-splitting. She was almost as excited as if she had won the gold medal herself.

And who knew, maybe one day she would... Simone loved to fantasise about competing in the Olympics. She even imagined what leotards she would wear to represent her country, and in her spare time she loved designing her own styles. Pinned to Simone's bedroom wall was her favourite quote from five-time Olympic gold medallist Nadia Comăneci – the first ever gymnast to be awarded a perfect score at the Olympics:

'Jump off the beam, flip off the bars, follow your dreams and reach for the stars.'

Looking at those words helped Simone remember the promise she'd made to herself in her diary all those months ago: 'I want to go the furthest I can.'

CHAPTER 6

HER FIRST CHEQUE

Making plans for the future was becoming increasingly important for Simone. It was a useful distraction from the present, where she was struggling.

When her family moved house, Ron and Nellie enrolled Simone in a new school, just across the road from Bannon's. The good news was that this made it easy for Simone to train before school and then return later in the afternoon for another practice session.

The bad news, however, was that Simone was unhappy in her new school. The other children were unfriendly and she didn't like her new teachers either. She missed laughing and joking around with her old friends, and soon she found herself seeking refuge in the gym. It was the only place where she felt fully able to be herself. Even if she didn't belong at school, at least Simone knew she belonged here with Aimee always pushing her up to the next level.

'I think you're ready for Houston, Simone,' Aimee told her, after a training session one day.

Simone beamed. The Houston National Invitational would be her first level 10 competition. At 13 years old, she'd be competing against 652 gymnasts of varying ages. But she didn't feel nervous, she felt excited. She always loved the thrill of competition.

And it was no different when the event came around. Simone could feel the audience watching her intently as she leapt and jumped her way around the beam. She heard their sharp intake of breath as she stuck each landing, with no forward or backward sway across the vault and floor. Cheers filled the hall as her scores came up on the board. She'd placed first on vault and floor, and third all-around.

Aimee hugged her. 'Congratulations, Simone. You've won $5000 dollars for Bannon's!' she said, proudly.

'Wow! Really?'

'Yes, I'm afraid the winnings have to go your gym programme, rather than you personally, so you can't touch it. If you accept money for a performance it means you've turned pro and can't compete in college.'

Well, Simone definitely did not want to jeopardise her chances of being recruited by a university on a sports scholarship. Going to college one day was one of her dreams.

'It's as big as me!' she laughed as she stood next to the enormous cheque. She remembered Aimee's words though and did her best not to touch it, which was difficult when all the photographers were asking her to hold it while she posed.

'I can't touch it. My coach told me not to.'

The photographers looked confused – and so did her dad, Ron. 'Is there a problem, honey?' he asked, rushing to her side.

'They keep asking me to hold the cheque, but Aimee said I can't touch it because then I won't have a chance to compete in college.'

Ron's face softened and he chuckled. 'Oh bless you, Simone. Aimee didn't mean it literally. You can't accept the money, but it's ok for you to touch it.'

Simone went bright red. 'Okay, thanks, Dad.'

'Hey, you've had a long day, don't worry about it!' he smiled.

Simone and her family teased her about her mistake for weeks to come. But Simone didn't mind, she was just glad she hadn't ruined her chances of being recruited for college gymnastics. Right now, all her dreams were important to her.

If only she could fast forward through middle school to get there quicker.

CHAPTER 7

ROLE MODELS

'Sit down, Simone. I have some news for you.'

Simone felt her stomach flutter. She'd known Aimee long enough to know that 'news' didn't always mean 'good news'.

'I'm afraid it's not the response we were hoping for.' In her hand she held a letter.

'It's from Márta Károlyi, isn't it?'

'Yes.' Aimee frowned. 'You're a magnificent tumbler, she's in no doubt of that. But she says you still need to progress on the bars before she'll help train you.'

Simone was devastated. Working with Martha

was key to progressing to elite gymnastics. And it was the uneven bars that were holding her back.

That night, she talked it over with Nellie. 'Mom, what do I need to do to get better on bars?'

'Perhaps it's time we looked for a new coach. Maybe Aimee doesn't have the skills to take you to an elite level.'

'But Mom, I like Aimee, she's practically family to me. Like you and Dad!'

'I know, honey, but if we're to get you to where you want to go...'

Simone sighed. She remembered the promise she had made to herself in her diary. As difficult as it would be, she agreed to let Nellie talk to Aimee.

'I appreciate your concerns,' said Aimee. 'I promise, if I ever think that I can't give Simone what she needs, I'll ask for help from other coaches.'

Nellie nodded. 'I know how much you care about Simone. I'm glad we're all on the same page.'

Simone smiled with relief. She hated the thought of being coached by someone else. 'I really want to stay with Aimee, Mom,' she whispered.

'Then let's stick together,' said Nellie. 'Agreed?'

'Agreed,' said Aimee.

For the rest of the season, Aimee and Simone continued to work on strengthening Simone's performance on the bars. At just four feet eight inches, Simone was still small for a 14-year-old. And the uneven bars, towering above her, were still daunting.

'You're performing for a crowd,' Aimee reminded her. 'And yes, you will be judged. But remember what brought you to gymnastics – you love the feeling of flying through the air! Don't ever forget that you're here to enjoy this.'

Simone threw herself into training with ever greater drive and determination. She watched videos on repeat of gymnastic legends Shannon Miller and Dominique Dawes, who were part of the gold medal-winning Magnificent Seven team in Atlanta 1996. She poured over their routines and urged Aimee to teach her the trickier combination moves that held a higher difficulty rating value. She based her training sessions around the questions: 'How can I get where they are?' and 'What skills do they have that I don't?'

After each routine during practice – whether on bars, vault, beam or floor – Simone asked Aimee if she thought it was worth a score above 15. Anything above that number would normally fall within medal range. It was a helpful way for Simone to ensure she was blending difficulty and technicality with artistic flair.

Simone's dedication was paying off...

At the Junior Olympics Nationals in Dallas, she was crowned US Challenge Pre-Elite All-Around Champion for 2010. From the podium, Simone and Aimee grinned at each other. Surely it wouldn't be long until they got the call from Márta Károlyi?

But, for now, there was the small matter of Simone's very first elite competition: the Gliders National Elite Qualifier in Riverside, California. Simone would be performing alongside some of the best young gymnasts in the country.

The pressure was on and Simone's nerves were really kicking in...

'What's going on? I'm not usually this nervous,' she asked Aimee in alarm.

'Nerves are normal. If you're not at all nervous before a competition, something's wrong,' Amy reassured her. 'What are you most concerned about, Simone? I'm sure you'll ace the floor. You always do.'

'The vault. I want my landing to be as faultless as possible.'

'Why don't you try some visualisation,' Aimee suggested. 'See in your mind's eye just how you want your performance to go. Do it before you fall asleep at night or just before you perform the routine. It will help calm your nerves.'

As Simone waited on the run-up to the vault, she put Aimee's advice into practice. Although she looked confident in her black and white leotard, with her hair swept back into a high bun, inside, her stomach was churning. As she waited for the judge to raise the flag, she visualised herself hitting the springboard, spinning through the air and sticking her landing effortlessly.

Now to make it a reality...

As soon as the flag was raised, Simone took a deep breath and sped off along the runway. Before she'd even hit the vault, she knew her handspring entry was flawless. From there, she soared into a double twist and felt her feet land perfectly on the mat.

'Yes!' She looked over to Aimee, who grinned back.

Next up, the uneven bars. Would the weeks of focused training pay off?

Simone got through her basic without error. Phew! The cheers of the crowd gave her a glow of pride.

The balance beam was next and Simone wobbled a little as she performed handsprings and half twists, but she didn't fall.

But it was as she bounded across the mat to take her first tumble on the floor, that she could feel the atmosphere in the hall change. Out of the corner of her eye, she could see the audience craning their necks to get a better view, and she could hear the sound of people's voices growing quieter.

'They all stopped and stared when you were tumbling,' said Aimee, proudly, as she high-fived her.

'Was it enough, though? My bar and beam weren't that great.' Simone looked worried.

But as the final scores were posted – 'First on vault and all-around!' exclaimed Aimee.

'There must be a mistake!' cried Simone, shocked and thrilled at the same time.

'No mistake!' replied Aimee, pulling her into a hug. 'It was better than you think! If you keep going like this you can make this year's national junior team.'

Simone's face lit up – her dream of competing for her country was a step closer.

A week later, Aimee called Simone into her office. There was a big smile on her face.

'Guess who's invited you to train with her?'

'Martha? Yes!' Simone let out a whoop of delight. She flung her arms around Aimee and the two of them jumped up and down together. Now that she was firmly on Martha's radar, a world of possibility opened up. Elite gymnastics? The national team? Even – Simone hardly dared dream – the Olympic Games?

'You've worked so hard,' Aimee told her. 'You deserve this.'

'It's your dream too,' Simone reminded her with a laugh. 'And I'm not going to let you down!'

CHAPTER 8

NAILING THE TKATCHEV

Martha's expression was stern as she surveyed the lines of gymnasts.

'We strive for perfection here,' she said. 'If that's not your goal, then you're in the wrong place.'

Simone looked down at her feet, a little intimidated. The strict atmosphere of the training centre here was so unlike Simone's light-hearted practice sessions with Aimee. Training began at eight in the morning and went on till seven at night, and the drills and body-conditioning work were relentless. Simone wasn't used to repeating a move what felt like 90 times over – she got bored too quickly for that! She looked around her at the determination on the other girls' faces. Like them, she needed to stay focused. This wasn't supposed to be fun. It wasn't supposed to be easy. She longed to lighten the mood by cracking a joke, but she knew Martha was watching every move.

It was going to be a long week. But in her heart, Simone knew it was the challenge she needed if she wanted to progress.

Luckily, once the sessions were over for the day, there was time to relax. Simone struck up close friendships with the other gymnasts: Courtney Collins, Nia Dennis and Destinee Davis. They played swing ball together or wandered around the grounds, gazing in amazement at the peacocks, camels and donkeys that roamed freely.

After a few days, Simone felt a little less intimidated by Martha's strictness. But she still struggled to keep a straight face during the endless drills – especially when Martha lined them up in height order. Simone was always last in line, of course!

The week at the centre was a gruelling one for Simone and her new friends, but the hard work soon paid off. A few weeks later, Simone competed in the American Classic, an annual summer gymnastics meet for elite female artistic gymnasts. She took first on vault and balance beam and third all-around. With a final score of 53.650, she had qualified for the Visa National Championships that August. It was here that Martha would be making her selection for the junior national team...

But Simone had a problem. If she was going to get selected, she still needed improvement on the bars. There was one move in particular that continued to bamboozle her: the Tkatchev, named after the world-famous male gymnast, Aleksandr Tkatchev, who invented it.

'I'm never going to get it right!' she moaned to Aimee, at a training session with her. She had fallen from the bars the first time she had tried the Tkatchev and now she couldn't shake the fear of injuring herself.

'Remember how you struggled with the giant, Simone?' said Aimee.

Simone nodded. Aimee was reminding her not to give up. 'Can we go through it again?'

'Before you reach the top, release your hands from the bar, spin in mid-air, then catch the bar on the other side.'

But the Tkatchev continued to test Simone. She kept falling to the mat each time she released the bar.

'It's all about timing,' explained Aimee. 'The trick is pinpointing exactly when to catch the bar on the way round – if you grab it too early, you smack into the bar; if you're late, you'll miss it completely.'

'I just can't do it! Whatever we're doing isn't working!' said Simone, panicked.

'Keep trying. You can do this,' said Aimee, patiently.

'Release and catch, release and catch,' Simone told herself.

But still she kept on slipping and falling, and

her frustration grew and grew. She wasn't used to failure!

With just a few minutes to go before the end of the session, Simone felt close to giving up. 'One more go,' she thought. 'Just one more. I'm doing it this time.'

And, without thinking, she swung round, released the bar, did a somersault in mid-air and caught the bar on the other side.

'You did it!' whooped Aimee. 'Well done, Simone! Great job!'

Tears of joy were running down Simone's face. Her perseverance had been worth it. 'Now I've done it once, Aimee, I know I can do it again!'

'How about we add it into your routine for the CoverGirl?' suggested Aimee. The CoverGirl Classic was another annual summer gymnastics meet. 'It'll be good practice for the National Championships later in the year,' she added.

Simone knew that if she wanted to perform the Tkatchev in competition, she would need to be able to do it right every time. Suddenly, she felt nervous again. 'Do you think I can?'

Aimee nodded. 'You can do anything you set your mind to. We need to start making your bar routines more difficult.'

The following week, negative thoughts began to swirl through Simone's head. She tried to visualise the perfect Tkatchev as Aimee had taught her, but instead she saw herself missing the bar and falling to the mat, crashing down in front of all the other elite gymnasts who could perform the manoeuvre effortlessly.

The day of the CoverGirl meet had arrived and the gymnasts were doing their final warm-ups. Simone felt panic rising in her chest. She was still missing the bar on the Tkatchev.

'I can't do this!' a voice in her head was shouting. 'I'm going to fail!'

She rushed from the hall into the bathroom. Staring at herself in the mirror, she burst into tears. 'What am I going to do?'

'Are you okay?'

Simone heard a voice from one of the cubicles. She recognised it as Lexie Priessman's. Simone had never spoken to Lexie before, but she had seen her win the all-around title at the Nastia Liukin Supergirl Cup in Worcester, Massachusetts the year before. Lexie was an amazing gymnast!

As Lexie emerged from the cubicle, Simone desperately dabbed at the smudges of mascara around her eyes. 'It's the Tkatchev. I didn't catch it once today. I've practised it over and over. I'm going to fail!'

The tears were streaming down her face again.

Lexie gave her a big smile. 'Ah yes, the Tkatchev. Well, we've all had problems with that. Do you know what helped me?'

Simone looked up at her.

'Let go of the bar much earlier, even if it feels wrong. You'll feel like it's too soon, but it works for me every time.'

Simone smiled through her tears. 'I'll give it a

try. Thank you!'

Simone still felt nervous as she walked out with the other competitors, but Lexie's kind advice had lifted her spirits. She shot a look towards the stands where Nellie, Ron and Adria were watching. The thought of their unwavering love and support always made her feel calmer.

'Okay,' thought Simone, 'you can do this.' She tried to ignore the churning feeling in her stomach as she lifted herself up on to the bar. 'Take it easy, it's just a bar. You can let go of it, and easily catch it again.'

Then the moment for the Tkatchev came. 'Okay, round I go...' Remembering Lexie's advice, Simone let go of the bar sooner than usual, propelled herself into mid-air, flipped over the bar and... caught it on the other side!

She'd done it!

Simone was so surprised she'd caught the bar that she faltered on the rest of her routine. She fell twice on moves she'd never had a problem with before. But she didn't care. By the time she finished her routine, she was beaming. She had nailed the dreaded Tkatchev and mastered her fears!

Aimee and Lexie both bounded over to congratulate her.

'I did it. I caught my Tkatchev!'

She was getting closer to achieving her dream of being chosen for the USA women's junior team.

CHAPTER 9

ONE POINT

Simone was bubbling with excitement as she arrived for her next practice session. With her fear of the Tkatchev out of the way, she was looking forward to finalising the details of her routine for the 2011 Visa National Championships. She knew she could improve it. She felt confident she could turn a good performance into a perfect one.

But she could tell from the serious look on Aimee's face that she had some important news. 'Martha's been in touch.'

'Oh?' Simone's heart skipped a beat.

'She wants to see you perform the Amanar at the

Nationals,' Aimee explained.

Simone's face fell. Named after Simona Amânar, who'd invented it, the Amanar was one of the hardest vault skills in the world.

Simone felt a rising panic as she ran through the movements in her head: a back handspring entry and two and a half twists in mid-air.

'Aimee, I don't feel ready. And we've always agreed, haven't we, it's better to be safe, rather than risk an injury?'

Aimee nodded. 'I'll support you in whatever you decide.'

'I know I can do an amazing Yurchenko instead!' said Simone. The Yurchenko was another very difficult move. 'Surely that will impress Martha?'

But on the day of the Championships, as Simone waited in line to perform, she began to wonder. Maybe she should have had a go at the Amanar? She was surrounded by elite competitors who weren't afraid to take on the toughest challenges.

With each event, Simone's doubts grew – and so did her nerves. She'd felt confident about the Yurchenko but landed badly. All the while, she was scolding herself for not attempting the Amanar.

Finally, the competition was over, and Simone held her breath as she lined up with the other gymnasts. All eyes were glued to the huge scoreboard, high above the arena. Only the 13 highest-scoring girls would make the national team. Simone knew there were plenty of girls who had done better. She wouldn't be at the top of the leader board. But she held her breath, waiting and hoping to see her name appear below the leaders.

Simone cheered along with the rest of the arena as the name of the girl with the highest score appeared: Katelyn Ohashi. The girls around Simone gave each other hugs of congratulations as their names appeared, and she kept smiling as the list continued, but, inside, she was beginning to panic. Where was her name? They were almost at the bottom of the list. Ten, eleven, twelve names were showing...

Finally, the 13th name appeared: Madison Desch. Just below, in 14th place: Simone Biles, one point below Madison. Simone had missed the team by just one point!

Simone felt like her world was crumbling. She'd had one goal and she'd failed to achieve it. As the jubilant atmosphere in the arena grew, Simone felt as though she was in a bad dream. She gritted her teeth. 'Don't let anyone see you cry,' she told herself. 'Not here.'

But back in her hotel room, she couldn't hold in her feelings any longer. She flung herself on her bed and burst into tears.

Nellie and Ron took turns to hold her tight, stroking her hair and whispering words of comfort. 'You came so close, Simone. You're still only a junior. We're so proud of what you achieved today.'

But Simone couldn't shake the feeling of having let everyone down. Her parents, her coaches and, of course, herself. In her head, she ran over and over her routines, with every small mistake seeming bigger every time.

Suddenly the phone rang and Simone heard her mom answer. 'Hi Ron Junior! Simone, it's your brother.'

Simone knew her brothers, Ron Junior and Adam, had been watching her performance back home because the National Championships were televised. Her heart sank at the thought that her whole family – the whole country – had watched her fail.

Nellie held out the phone. 'He wants to speak to you, honey.'

'Hello?'

'Hey Simone! Now listen. I know you are disappointed right now, and that today wasn't the result you'd dreamt of, but trust me, your dreams are not over. Not by a long stretch,' Ron Junior said. 'You missed by one point – one! You're so close to making the team. Next time it'll be your turn.'

Tears were rolling down Simone's cheeks again. Right now, that seemed impossible.

Ron Junior could hear how upset she was. 'Please, don't beat yourself up. Maybe this is the motivation you need to train even harder. Today may not be your day, but it will come. We all know how good you are and we all believe in you.'

Simone's sobs began to subside.

'We're all so proud of you!'

She managed to say in a small voice: 'Thanks so much, Ron, that's sweet of you to say.'

'It's the truth, Simone.'

Simone felt a huge weight lift from her shoulders as she put the phone down. Maybe she was putting too much pressure on herself? She was the first gymnast from Bannon's to ever compete at the Nationals. She had been only one point away from achieving a place on the national team. Today had felt like the end of everything – but perhaps it was only the beginning.

As Ron Junior had said it would, this small failure

made Simone determined to work even harder.

And back at Bannon's, it didn't take long for her coaches to raise the issue of the Amanar.

The head coach went straight to the point. 'You didn't make the team because you didn't try that move. It would have pushed up your difficulty rating by a long shot.'

Back at the competition, Simone had been angry at herself for not attempting the Amanar. But now, she remembered what Nellie always told her. 'Don't go against your instincts, Simone. Set your own limits and be confident in them.'

'It didn't feel right,' she said simply.

'What are you thinking about when you perform, Simone?'

'I'm thinking about whether or not I'm as good as the other girls.'

Aimee frowned. 'Simone, you need to stop comparing yourself to others. You are as good. Often better. You just need to believe it. Such negative thoughts will affect your performance.'

Simone agreed. She knew she had a habit of overthinking. When her mind began to whirr, she would feel her muscles tighten and nervous energy would bubble up inside her. When that happened, mistakes often followed.

It was clear to Aimee that though Simone was every bit as good as the other gymnasts, they still needed to work to increase the level difficulty of her routines in order to achieve higher scores. Together, they looked at videos of her events and identified the skills across each apparatus that she needed to work on.

'You have so much power, Simone,' said Aimee. 'But we need to make sure we can control it. Every time you hop on a landing, you lose points. The bigger the hop, the bigger the deduction.'

Simone grimaced. Her landings were often her weak point. 'Well, then I need to get better. I don't want to miss out making the team again.'

'You're going to need more time in the gym. We need to get you to the point where your skills are so rock solid that you're doing them in your sleep.'

Simone didn't know how she was going to fit more hours in.

'Have a think about it,' Aimee said gently. 'You've got a big decision ahead.'

Simone nodded. She knew exactly what Aimee meant. Normal teenage life versus elite gymnastics. Her heart felt heavy at the prospect of having to make a choice.

CHAPTER 10

SACRIFICE

Simone was due to start high school at the end of August, and there she would be reunited with her best friend, Marissa. All summer she'd been excited at the prospect of deciding what clubs to join and going to football games together. She'd even planned her outfit for her first day. But she still had to face her difficult decision. While it was possible to train 35 hours a week during the holidays, it would be almost impossible when she went back to school. If she chose gymnastics, she would have to be home-schooled.

It was the hardest choice Simone had ever had to

make. Elite gymnastics. Making the national team. A chance of competing at the Olympics. The joy she felt when she mastered a new routine. The cheers of the crowd as they watched her show off her skills.

Or the fun and normality of high school. Spending time with her friends. Being a regular teenager.

'Only you can make this decision, Simone,' her mom would tell her. But Simone was fed up of hearing this. She knew she was the only one who could decide – she just couldn't make up her mind.

Her dad tried to help. 'If you want to make the national team, you'll miss a lot of school when you go to monthly team camps. I can't see your new school letting you do that.'

Nellie added, 'But if you've got your heart set on school, gymnastics will have to take a back seat.'

'I want to do both!'

Her parents looked at each other. It wasn't like Simone to have tantrums. They didn't like to see her under so much pressure. And time was running out...

'You need to make your decision by Sunday, Simone,' said her mother. 'That's the deadline for high school enrolment.'

Simone flung down her cutlery and ran out of the room.

She lay on her bed and wept tears of frustration. Aimee had always explained she'd need to make sacrifices if she wanted to go the furthest she could in gymnastics. And, secretly, Simone knew what her decision would be, even if she wasn't ready to admit it to herself.

There was a knock on her door. 'Simone?' It was Nellie, firm but gentle. 'We understand, Simone, we get it. You're feeling sad you might miss out on high school. That's perfectly normal,' she said.

Although she felt cross, Simone couldn't help but love Nellie's ability to know what was going on in her mind.

'Whatever you choose, we're behind you, honey.'

Simone sighed. She thought of what her dad always said to her. 'God has given you a gift, Simone. Don't waste that gift.'

She looked her mom in the eye and took a deep breath. 'Ok, let's try home-schooling.'

Nellie's face broke out into a smile. 'That's great news, Simone. Well done for making the decision.'

Ron appeared at the top of the stairs, looking relieved. 'You'll always be top of the class now, honey!'

Simone managed to crack a smile, something she'd not done in a while. 'So who is going to be teaching me?'

Nellie and Ron looked at each other. They had agreed in advance who would give lessons to Simone if she chose this route.

'Your dad will be your teacher.'

Simone smiled. 'Thanks, Dad.' She knew she wasn't the only one making a sacrifice.

However, after six weeks studying together, and one terrible report card, it was clear that the teacher and pupil dynamic wasn't working.

'Let's try someone outside the family!' Nellie suggested.

So they hired a tutor called Miss Heather. Within a few months, Simone was settling into a routine and her grades were shooting up. Perhaps home-schooling wasn't so bad, after all.

But in the gym, the long hours of training were beginning to take their toll. Simone was tired. The fun had gone out of it, and so had her motivation.

'Simone – get back up on the beam now and do the routine!'

'I did finish the routine!' Simone protested.

'You're not making the connections. You paused between the handsprings,' replied Aimee.

Simone groaned in frustration.

'I barely paused for a second!'

'That's enough to lose points, and you know it. Your connections need to be seamless.'

Simone tried another tactic. 'I've got a cold.'

'Well, go blow your nose, then come back and

get on the beam.'

As Simone stomped off to the toilet, she knew her attitude was off. If she continued, she knew Aimee would phone her parents: a last resort when Simone refused to do something. But she was fed up with training more than 35 hours a week in the gym. She wasn't having any fun. She was exhausted.

'Finished blowing your nose?' Aimee asked when she returned.

Simone glared at her.

'Talk it out, Simone, come on, what's up?'

'You're just making me go over and over and over stuff.'

'No, Simone, I'm making you do the work you need to do.'

'Yeah, well, maybe I'm just fed up with people telling me what to do.'

Aimee's jaw tightened. 'Are you still mad you're not going to high school?'

Simone thought for a minute. Yes, maybe she was.

She certainly didn't feel like a normal teenager.

'I get it, things would be a lot easier if you'd made a different choice. This feels like hard work, right?'

Simone nodded.

'It will be worth it. I promise. It just may not always feel that way. I don't think you'll regret your decision though. Not when you're standing at the top of a podium.'

'I'm just exhausted, Aimee,' Simone said quietly.

Aimee smiled. 'I know.'

'Sometimes I'd just like to go home and watch *Modern Family.*' It was one of her favourite shows.

'There's plenty of time for that. For now, get back on the bar, Simone.'

'Aimee?'

'Yeah?'

'Thanks for not calling my parents.'

'Don't count your chickens too soon, young lady – let's see how the rest of the session goes!'

Simone got back on the beam and ran through

10 routines, making all her connections. She had grown to appreciate Aimee's training techniques. Her coach knew instinctively when to keep pushing Simone to try harder. But she also understood when Simone was genuinely exhausted and needed to rest.

And though Simone might complain, nothing could quite equal the joy of flying though the air.

Deep down, she knew it was worth the sacrifice. She had made the right decision.

CHAPTER 11

RAISING HER GAME

With the extra training Aimee was providing, Simone's confidence was growing every day. Even the complicated two and a half twist on the Amanar no longer phased her.

'Don't worry that you can't see the vault when you round off onto the board, trust that it's there and that it's got you,' Aimee told her.

Simone's technique was improving all the time, as was her ability to control her body's natural power. By now she knew her routines so well that she could practically perform them in her sleep, as long as she kept her other fears at bay.

'You see, Simone, gymnastics is about patience. It's not just about throwing the big flamboyant moves.' Aimee smiled.

Simone now had the chance to prove herself in front of Márta Károlyi at the American Classic. If she did well there, she'd qualify for the Visa National Championships in Huntsville at the end of the season. That meant she had a chance for a spot on the 2012 national women's junior team.

But the night before the event, as Simone chose which leotard to wear, Nellie could see she was distracted.

'Simone, is there something on your mind?'

Simone sidestepped the question. 'No, not really.'

Nellie knew better. 'You're more than ready to perform amazingly tomorrow. But if there's something on your mind, it could block you doing the best you can. So talk to me.'

Simone sighed. 'I suppose it's... the girls.'

'The other girls you're competing against?'

'Yes.'

Her mom's face darkened. 'Is someone being mean to you?'

'No, the opposite! I think that's the problem. I really like them!'

'So...'

'Well, maybe they won't like me if I do really well.'

Her mother put her arm around her. 'Simone, of course they won't stop liking you. You've all worked hard to get where you are. You all spur each other on to do better.'

It was true. Gymnasts like Lexie Priessman and Katelyn Ohashi encouraged Simone to work harder and raise her game.

'But remember, Simone, the most important thing is to perform your very best. Don't go out there to beat anyone. If your best performance is the best to win the competition that day, then that's how it should be. If it means you finish last, well, hey, so be it. Go out there and be the best Simone that you can be.'

As she took in Nellie's words, Simone felt as though another weight had lifted from her shoulders. And when she entered the arena the following day, her mind was clear and free from worry. Last year, she'd not felt confident enough to attempt the Amanar. Now, here she was, having overcome her fears, and about to perform it to the best of her ability.

Be the best Simone that you can be. Her mom's words rang in her ears.

As she took her run-up, she knew she'd created just the right amount of power to propel her body off the vault and through the air into the difficult two and a half twists. Her face broke into a huge smile as she stuck her landing and the crowd cheered. She'd nailed it! She'd nailed the Amanar!

And the judges agreed. Simone's eyes widened as she took in the final scores. 'First place on vault!'

Aimee high-fived her. 'You've worked so hard for that.'

In June, Simone triumphed again on vault, taking

first place at the Nationals in St Louis, Missouri. She also placed third in all-around, which meant she had a place on the podium next to gold medallist Lexie Priessman and silver medallist Madison Desch. She couldn't stop smiling as she stood on her plinth with a bronze medal around her neck, holding her bouquet of flowers high in the air.

And there was more to come. Martha was yet to announce the names of the women's junior national team; this year she would only be choosing six. As the names flashed up on the screen, Simone felt as though she'd explode with happiness. There was her name, alongside five other girls who'd all made the team the previous year: Lexie Preissman, Madison Desch, Bailie Key, Katelyn Ohashi and Amelia Hundley.

'The only newbie!' said Aimee, squeezing her shoulders. 'I'm so proud of you, Simone.'

The junior national team! As Simone lined up to be photographed with the rest of the team, she felt as though everything was falling into place at last.

CHAPTER 12

LONDON 2012

It was 2012 and the Olympic Games in London were in full swing. Simone and the other gymnasts at Bannon's gathered excitedly around the large screen set up in the gym. They were watching the US gymnastics team, nicknamed the Fierce Five, battle it out for gold against Russia and China. Not since the Magnificent Seven in 1996 had the country's women gymnasts taken gold in the Games. First, though, they would have to see off tough competition from Russia's Viktoria Komova and Romania's Sandra Isbasa.

'Wow!' Simone and her friends gasped in unison

as the USA's Gabby Douglas showed off her finesse in the floor exercise. A dazzling array of twists and jumps left them speechless. They held their breaths as she spun and jumped her way through her bar and beam routines to take gold for individual all-around.

Following Gabby's lead, Team USA was destined for gold that year. Chills went up and down Simone's spine as she watched the Fierce Five standing on the podium for the medal ceremony, their hands on their hearts as they sang 'The Star Spangled Banner'. She tried to imagine how it felt to stand on the podium with your teammates, knowing that you'd all worked together to win gold for your country.

'That could be you, Simone!' Simone was jolted out of her daydream by a voice behind her. 'What?'

'You! You'll be on that podium in four years.'

Before she knew it, all the girls were chanting, 'Simone for Rio! Simone for Rio! You're gonna do it! That's gonna be you!'

'Oh, whatever guys,' Simone laughed it off.

But as she watched Team USA celebrate their win, she couldn't help daydreaming. Rio was still four years away and Simone preferred to focus on short term goals. But why not? Maybe it was possible. In that moment, she quietly asked God to help her do everything within her power to be part of the 2016 Olympics team.

CHAPTER 13

SWEET SIXTEEN

Simone was having a blast at Nationals Camp. She was striking up close friendships with the team – the girls she'd admired from afar, like Katelyn, were now her peers.

'As a first senior assignment, this is pretty special,' said Aimee.

Simone knew it – in fact, her stomach knotted with anxiety every time she thought of the big crowd the event would draw, not to mention the TV coverage.

'Remember to have fun,' Aimee reminded her.

But fun was easier said than done. On the day

of the competition, Simone felt sick with nerves. The thought of letting Martha down, when she'd taken such a big chance on choosing her for the Nationals team, was overwhelming.

'Come on Simone, you can do this,' she said to herself as she prepared for the vault.

Simone sailed through the air and performed a perfect Amanar.

It was on the beam that she ran into problems. Misjudging her footing on a backward flip sequence, she found herself crashing to the floor. As she lay on the mat in stunned shock, she struggled to keep the tears back.

'Simone, you must finish your routine,' she told herself. Finishing the routine was the golden rule. She got back up onto the beam and aced the dismount, with the audience clapping her encouragingly.

But all Simone could think of was failing in front of everyone on her first assignment. Martha was going to be mad! Was her career over before it had even begun?

She hurried off the mat, desperate to find a quiet corner where she could let her feelings out. But there were reporters following her. Camera lenses were zooming into her face. There was nowhere to hide! Nowhere to cry!

But to Simone's surprise, her fears were unfounded. Martha wasn't in the slightest bit angry.

'Simone, look at the scores – you've come second! Silver in the American Cup is a huge achievement. I'm proud of you. You just need to get a little more confident on the beam.' Martha smiled down at her, her brown eyes twinkling. 'There's nothing wrong with your gymnastics. Your self-belief just needs a little sorting out.'

A wave of relief swept over Simone. It was true. She was putting up barriers for herself by believing that she wasn't good enough.

Well, she was determined to change that!

2013 was an exciting year for Simone. She travelled to Europe for her first international camp with the US team. Here she took first in vault, beam, floor exercise and individual all-around. It was also the year she turned 16 and her parents bought her the car of her dreams: a turquoise-blue Ford Focus. She was overjoyed to see it sitting waiting for her in the garage, although it wasn't complete for her until she'd lined it with a zebra-patterned interior.

Her dad shook his head when he saw it. 'I've got to drive around in this, have I?'

She grinned. 'Well yeah, Dad. If you're going to give me lessons.'

Simone was clearly in the driving seat, however, when it came to steering her elite, senior gymnastics career to success. She had to pinch herself that she'd come so close to gold at the American Cup and was now competing against Olympic champions Aly Raisman and Gabby Douglas.

But over the next few weeks, Aimee noticed a

difference in Simone. She didn't seem to be trying as hard. She wasn't listening as carefully. And when she refused to re-do a routine for the third time, Aimee could no longer ignore her troubling new attitude.

'What's going on? Has the Simone I know and love gone on holiday or something?'

Simone frowned. 'I don't see why I have to keep doing the same thing, that's all.'

'You can't just pull a medal-winning performance out of the hat every time. You need to be consistent,' Aimee reminded her.

'Well, I seem to have managed it so far,' Simone replied, flippantly.

Aimee looked at her in shock. 'Er, young lady, you need to keep training if you want to keep winning, trust me. You're going to fall flat on your face soon if you don't.'

And Simone was about to find out just how literal Aimee's prediction was.

It was July and she was about to take to the bars

at the US Secret Classic meet. Aimee and Martha were watching from the sidelines, and out of the corner of her eye, Simone could see a look of concern on Martha's face.

If Simone was honest, she wasn't feeling right. She felt tired. Her limbs and muscles weren't feeling as strong as usual. The night before, Aimee had told her it was because she hadn't practised enough.

Simone put Aimee's words to the back of her mind as she started her routine. But within seconds, she was in trouble. As she flung herself backwards over the bar to perform the Tkatchev, she fell and landed with a gasp on the mat. It was the first time she'd missed the catch in years. She heard a sharp intake of breath from the audience and saw a look of bewilderment on Martha's face.

She hopped back up to try it for the second time. This time she performed it perfectly, but it didn't matter: she couldn't put her mistake out of her mind and fumbled her way through the rest of the routine.

By the time she got to the floor exercise, she couldn't get enough height to pull off a rotation in the air and landed awkwardly on one of her ankles.

'I'm making such a mess of this,' she thought. 'I'm completely humiliating myself.'

Feeling furious with herself, she walked over to her final event, the vault. But Aimee pulled her aside. 'I'm taking you out of the competition.' Her tone was harsh.

'No!' Simone hissed back.

'You're going to injure yourself if you continue performing like this.'

Simone shrugged and stormed off, pretending she didn't care. But immediately she ran into Martha, whose stern face told Simone everything she needed to know.

'You're a senior now, Simone. And I think we both know that that was not the performance of a senior. You only have yourself to blame. You haven't taken this seriously enough. Let this be a lesson to you. You return to the gym and you work hard and prepare hard, like I know you can.'

Simone couldn't look her in the eye. She knew Martha was right and she felt ashamed.

It was only three weeks until the Nationals and she vowed to make up for her poor performance in the time she had left. She owed it to everyone, and especially herself, to try her hardest.

CHAPTER 14

VALUABLE LESSONS

'What do you love so much about gymnastics, Simone?'

'It's fun. Flying through the air is fun,' said Simone, without a moment's hesitation.

Simone was sitting in the office of Mr Andrews, a sports psychologist. Her parents had arranged a session to help Simone with her performance, her fears and worries.

'Were you having fun at the Secret Classic?' was his next question.

She shook her head.

'Why not?'

She sighed. 'I feel like there's a lot of expectation on me. When I'm out there, it's all I can focus on.'

'Okay. Did you start doing gymnastics for other people?'

'No.'

'Why did you start doing it?'

'Because it was fun.'

'So go out there with fun as your main focus. Don't go out there carrying the weight of what others expect or want from you,' he said. 'Promise me.'

Fun. That was all she needed to hear.

'Thank you,' Simone grinned. 'I promise.'

By the time the Nationals came around, she felt excited at the thought of competing. She had trained hard and felt relaxed about her routine. Once again, twisting, turning and flying through the air felt like the best fun in the world.

Simone's heart soared as she saw her scores flash up for each event. She won gold for all-around champion and silver across the four events. The difficulties of the past few months had been worth it: she'd learnt valuable lessons about herself.

And at the end of the meet came the best news of all. Alongside Brenna Dowell, McKayla Maroney, Kyla Ross and Elizabeth Price, Simone had been chosen for the US national senior team to compete in the World Championships in Belgium in September. Her first international competition!

Under Martha's watchful eye, the girls spent the summer training together. Team spirit was everything, Martha explained. 'You need to have each other's backs when you're performing. You'll fall apart as a team otherwise.'

Simone embraced bonding with the girls outside the gym as much as she enjoyed practising their routines together. They swapped make-up tips, hilarious ideas for leotards and invented games to help wile away long, rainy afternoons.

While Simone prepared for her first World Championships alongside her new teammate, she remembered the promise she'd made to Mr Andrews. Whenever she began to feel the pressure of other people's expectations, she found ways to relax. Top of her list was her turtle figurine collection. She'd started collecting these little turtles when she first went to Belize, her mom's home country, and now she always remembered to pick out a new one wherever she travelled in the world.

She loved the freedom they represented; they carried their weight but they carried it lightly. They were a reminder that she needed to do the same. Having the turtles with her when she went to competitions helped her to feel calm. It had become her special tradition to bring at least six turtles with her wherever she went. She always took her luckiest, which had a little red ladybug on its back.

The weight of people's expectations needn't be a burden, she reminded herself. She was so lucky to have the love and support of her friends, her family, her coaches!

CHAPTER 15

THE BILES

The World Championships were due to take place in Antwerp's Sports Palace. Over six days, Simone and her US teammates would perform alongside talented gymnasts from all across the world: from Romania's Larisa Iordache to Italy's Vanessa Ferrari and Russia's Aliya Mustafina. They were competing to become all-around individual champions and for separate titles on vault, uneven bars, beam and floor.

Simone was daunted at the prospect of her performance being beamed out across the world. She was about to go from being an 'unknown' to an

international gymnast. The idea was terrifying!

As she laid out her leotards the night before flying to Antwerp, she remembered Martha's advice from a few days before. 'You've nothing to lose and everything to gain at the Worlds. Take it one day at a time.'

And that's just what Simone did. Soaking up the atmosphere of the stadium, she perfectly tumbled and twisted her way through the qualifying rounds with a broad smile on her face.

At last it was the final of the all-around competition. Simone's first event was the vault. As usual, she gave a smile for the judges, before turning her gaze to the runway, a look of steely determination on her face. She remembered Aimee's words, just a few minutes before: 'There are still only a handful of gymnasts across the world who can perform the Amanar. It's the hardest vault in the world. Remember that.'

With that thought in her mind, she sped down the runway into a roundoff onto the springboard, into a backspring onto the vault and into a double and a half twist. She didn't quite stick her landing but she knew her form in the air and technique had made an impression on the audience, who roared their approval.

Had she won over the judges though?

Her heart raced as she waited for her score. Finally – yes! 15.80. It was a great start and put her ahead of the Russian Aliya Mustafina. Next up were the bars, where she performed the Weiler kip: a tricky move that gave her a high difficulty rating. She moved onto three Tkatchevs before ending her routine on a strong dismount where she stuck her landing. As she strode off the mat, she double high-fived Aimee. 'Amazing!' cried her coach. 'So proud of you!'

Simone was comfortably in the lead by now, but as she faced the beam, she felt her nerves rise. Beam had always been tricky for Simone. It required so much balance, and with so much power in her muscles it wasn't always easy for her to stay in control. But she began her routine impeccably, performing a stunning turn that she knew would impress the judges. A huge cheer went up from the crowd as she performed a full back twist into a solid dismount.

So far, so good!

Simone was still in the lead, but she had a difficult move to perform in floor exercise. In fact, it was one she'd invented herself! One day in training, Simone had strained a calf muscle on a backward landing during a double layout. Aimee didn't want her to strain it further, so she suggested a half twist at the end of the double flip in the air. The landing would be trickier but it would put less strain on Simone's calves. Martha liked the new combination and agreed that she should add it to her floor routine.

Aimee looked at her and grinned. 'No pressure but if you pull this off at Worlds, your move will become known as "The Biles."'

'And other gymnasts will start performing it?' Simone gulped. 'In competitions?'

'Exactly!'

The floor exercise was her last event that day but Simone could feel the energy flowing through her body as she walked into the arena. As she sprang effortlessly around the mat, she felt as though she could easily fly out of the boundaries – her legs felt so full of power! Her first tumble went without a hitch. But it was her second that would incorporate her new move. Could she pull off The Biles? With a huge smile on her face, she took an energetic run-up before flinging herself gracefully into the double layout with a half twist at the end.

'I've done it!'

Now her move would make it into the history books! Filled with pride, Simone flew through the rest of her routine as the audience clapped along. It ended with uproarious applause from the packed stadium.

But her jaw still fell open when she saw her name at the top of the scoreboard. With 60.216 points, Simone had won gold in individual all-around. She was the 2013 Artistic Gymnastics World Champion.

'Is this really happening?' She turned to Aimee, who was welling up.

'It is happening, Simone. You're World Champion.'

Up in the audience, she could see Nellie and Ron hugging as tears poured down their faces. But the performance was not over yet for Simone. She still had to receive her gold medal!

She turned to Aimee in a panic. 'I don't know what to do!'

'You're the gold medallist, so you need to shake everyone's hand.'

Simone felt like a complete newbie as she walked out with the eight other finishers, all making their way to the podiums. Ahead of her was Kyla, who'd taken silver, and Aliya Mustafina, who'd taken bronze. It was only the third time that the US had won the World Championship all-around gold and silver medals.

As she took her place on the top podium, Simone

was shaking so hard she thought she might topple – she wasn't sure if it was from joy, nerves or disbelief!

She thought back to the conversation she'd had with her dad, Ron, on the phone after narrowly missing out on making the junior team. He'd told her that her time would come and it had, sooner than she'd expected. She was so relieved she'd listened to him and not given up.

Over the next two days, Simone went on to win a silver medal in vault, bronze in beam and gold on floor. She left the competition with four medals in total. By now she looked like a pro as she took to the podium, smiling for the cameras and waving her bouquet.

But it wasn't until she returned home that the enormity of her success hit her. To celebrate her win, her parents threw a party with caterers and a DJ. After a while, Simone felt so overwhelmed she slipped away to her bedroom. As she sat on her bed, the smell of barbecued food and the sound of people laughing drifted up through her window. Just then one of her favourite songs came on: Ellie Goulding's 'Burn'. It took her straight back to training in the Sports Palace in Antwerp and reminded her of all the hard work she'd put in to become World Champion. She lay back on her bed and she cried tears of joy and pride.

Right now, with her World Championship medal by her bedside, friends and family celebrating outside, Simone felt like she had conquered the world.

CHAPTER 16

NEW CHALLENGES

'I'm afraid Aimee won't be working here at Bannon's any longer. She has decided to leave and won't be at the gym from now on.'

Simone's heart skipped a beat. She stared at Tomas, the coach who had made the announcement. Could it be true? Her beloved coach? Her most loyal supporter?

The other gymnasts looked at each other in shock. Aimee was nowhere to be seen. Simone knew she had to speak to her. Immediately. She rushed from the gym, scared that she might burst into tears.

But when she returned home, she found Aimee

and her mother talking together.

'Aimee! What's going on? Why are you leaving?' Simone's lips trembled. The tears were about to fall.

'I've decided to leave Bannon's. But I don't want to stop coaching you.'

Simone's mother asked: 'Where do you want to go?'

'I'm not sure yet,' replied Aimee. 'But I'd like you to come with me. I promise I won't let you down. It'll be somewhere with the best support, the best equipment.'

Simone knew one thing for sure: she wanted to carry on being coached by Aimee. The stakes were getting higher at each competition, but Aimee encouraged Simone to have fun, no matter how hard she trained. Simone knew Aimee always had her best interests at heart.

Nellie paused for a moment. 'How about I build a gym?'

Simone and Aimee's mouths fell open. 'Build

a gym?'

'Well, why not? It'll give my girls a safe and well-equipped place to train.'

Simone watched as Nellie pulled her laptop open. She could see the idea taking shape in her mom's head as she started looking for plots of land for sale in the area. By the time Ron arrived home, Nellie had found the perfect location.

'Ron, we're building a gym.'

'Building a gym?' He was slightly taken aback, but as soon as he saw the serious look on his wife's face, he knew better than to argue. 'Well, if you say so.'

Nellie's vision was clear: a family-friendly training gym that would offer classes in taekwondo, cheerleading and kickboxing, as well as competitive gymnastics. It would even have home-school classrooms. They would name it World Champions Centre.

Simone's parents threw themselves into the project immediately, hiring architects and builders.

But constructing a gym from scratch was a time-consuming and difficult project. As time went on, they realised it would take longer to complete than they'd originally thought. So they found two warehouse bays that they turned into a makeshift gym with the best equipment. Before long they had eight gymnasts training there. By the time the centre was ready, they knew there would be many more.

It was a difficult few months for Simone. In addition to the disruption, she was dealing with a shoulder injury from a handstand exercise during training at Nationals Camp. It meant she had to miss the first half of the 2014 competition season and cut down on her training time.

But by August 2014, Simone was thriving again. As she performed her medal-winning moves around the mat at the P&G National Championships in Pittsburgh, she knew her body was back in shape; she couldn't stop smiling as the crowd clapped and cheered along with her.

'I nailed that routine,' she thought to herself as

she left the mat.

And the judges agreed. She took gold on vault and floor and tied with Alyssa Baumann for silver on beam.

Based on that performance, she was chosen to compete at the World Championships again, this time in Nanning, China. Here, she would be defending her title from the previous year and it was difficult to put other people's expectations out of her mind.

Plus, she wasn't just competing as an individual this year. As the 2013 World Championships had happened so soon after the 2012 Olympics, there had been no team competition. This year, she was competing as Team USA for the first time, alongside Kyla Ross, Mykayla Skinner, Ashton Locklear, Madison Kocian and Alyssa Baumann. If any one of them made a mistake, it put the whole team's win at risk. As ever, they faced tough competition from the host-country, China, as well as Russia. On events, Simone knew she had to watch out for

Larisa Iordache and Russia's Aliya Mustafina, who always excelled on the uneven bars.

Simone was confident that she had a good blend of difficulty and execution on each of her routines, although she'd taken out a Tkatchev on her bar routine to reduce the risk of further injury to her shoulder.

She didn't make the event final for bars but took gold on floor exercise and silver on the vault. She also took gold for the beam, beating China's Bai Yawen by 0.067 points. But most importantly, she took gold on individual all-around, successfully defending her 2013 title.

'You're World Champion for a second year,' whooped Kyla. 'That's amazing!'

And this year, Simone knew exactly what to do when she was called to the floor to take her place with the other winners. She climbed onto the first-place podium to receive her medal and bouquet as the American anthem filled the arena. With her right hand over her heart, Simone turned to the flag and began to sing 'The Star-Spangled Spanner'. Larisa and Kyla, who'd taken silver and bronze respectively, were either side of her on the podium. As they reached the end of the anthem, Simone breathed a deep sigh of relief. She was ready to step down from the podium now, away from the gaze of the crowd and the flashing of the cameras.

However, nothing could have prepared her for what happened next. As the three medallists turned to face the arena again, Larisa leaned over and pointed at Simone's bouquet. 'There's a bee!'

Simone looked down and froze in horror. She'd been scared of bees ever since she was a child. She tried her best to control her rising panic, but as the large bee took flight towards her hand, she gasped out loud. The audience looked on in bewilderment as she shook her hand out in front of her. *Keep hold of the bouquet*, she told herself. She knew how disrespectful it would look to drop her flowers!

But the bee was not in the mood for flying away. Instead it buzzed towards her head. Simone couldn't hide her fear any longer. She jumped off the podium. 'It won't stop following me!' she cried out.

Kyla and Larisa were doing their best to contain their laughter as Simone ran around in circles to escape it. Finally, the bee gave up its chase and retreated back into her bouquet. This time, Simone threw the bouquet to the ground and the bee found a new home among Kyla's flowers. As Simone jumped back on to the podium, the three of them burst out laughing, while bemused photographers gathered in front of them.

'Well, that was a memorable medal ceremony,' they joked.

That evening, Ron Junior phoned. Before she could even say 'hello', her brother was howling with laughter.

'That's my girl! Trust you! Never mind that you're World Champion – there's a flipping bee in your bouquet!'

'I know, I know – I'm so embarrassed!' Simone

started to laugh all over again at the memory of it.

'No Simone, it's brilliant, let the world see who you are. I love you, sister!'

Simone smiled at that. Yeah, she wasn't someone to take anything too seriously, even gymnastics. And she was happy for everyone else to see that too. However, she asked everyone to check their bouquets during the medal ceremony for Team USA. They'd won gold and she didn't want any more embarrassing incidents to steal their thunder!

CHAPTER 17

MAKING HISTORY

Simone was scrolling through the messages in her Twitter feed. Throughout 2015, fans and supporters had been telling her she would become World Champion for the third time. If she did, she'd make history as the first American woman to do so.

Ron Junior looked over her shoulder at the tweets. 'No pressure then!'

Simone sighed.

He shook her gently. 'Come on, you're three-time US national champion and two-time World Champion, you can understand why people's expectations are high.'

'I know.'

'Remember, it's just another practice.'

It usually helped Simone to remember this when she was feeling the pressure. But this year, she was struggling to keep her energy and optimism up ahead of the Worlds. The Championships were being held in Glasgow and the team had arrived a week early to help them adjust to the time zones. They had been thrown immediately into a tough training regime and Simone felt exhausted. She was beginning to obsess over her routines and all the many things that could go wrong.

'Aimee, do you think I'll fall?' she asked her coach.

'Have you fallen in training?'

Simone grimaced. 'No, but what if I do on the actual day?'

'Please give your brain a rest, Simone,' Aimee said gently. 'Adrenaline is good, but not this much.'

But Simone couldn't relax – and just as Aimee had feared, it was starting to affect her performance. In the all-around final, in the middle of a front tuck on her bar routine, she began to topple.

'Grab on for dear life, Simone,' she told herself. 'Do not fall!'

She knew points would be deducted for holding onto the beam – though not as many as for falling. But despite her mistake, Simone was still top of the scoreboard. With a total score of 60.399, she took gold for the all-around, defending her World Champion title for the third year running. Her teammate, Gabby Douglas, took silver and Larisa Iordache took bronze.

Simone had made history. And as she fell into a deep sleep that night, she dreamt of flying home, hugging her family and finally stepping into the World Champions Centre her parents had opened. She knew how proud they were of her. She was so happy she had been able to give them something to celebrate!

***

Simone sat in the mall with her sister, drinking her favourite orange-flavoured smoothie. It was great spending time with Adria after so many weeks of travelling. But something wasn't right. She kept noticing people looking over at her. Simone looked down at her blouse to check she hadn't just spilt something all over herself.

'Adria, is it just me, or are people staring at us?'

Adria scoffed. 'They're staring at you, Simone, not me.'

'But... why?'

Adria looked at her as though she was a complete idiot. 'Oh come on.'

'What?'

Just then, a little girl with blonde hair walked cautiously over to Simone's table. 'Hi,' she said shyly.

'Hi!' Simone replied brightly. The girl's mother was standing just a few yards behind her, smiling.

'Are you Simone Biles?'

'Er, yes!'

'Could I take a picture with you?'

'Of course.' Simone smiled warmly, but inside she was still puzzled. Once the girl and her mother had thanked her and walked away, she turned to her sister. 'What was that about?'

Adria lost her patience. 'Are you kidding me?' she snapped. 'You're three-time World Champion!'

But Simone was still confused. She was simply sitting in the mall of her home-town, yet her love of flying through the air had brought her fans all over the world. Suddenly it all seemed so surreal!

'And I always thought my sister was just some gym nerd.'

They both started laughing, but there was pride in Adria's eyes.

CHAPTER 18

DIFFICULT CHOICES

Aimee looked Simone straight in the eye.

'I'm afraid this is another difficult decision you've got to make.'

She was at another fork in the road. She had wanted to study sports business at college and catch up on her lost high-school days, but she also had her eyes on the Olympics in Rio. Sponsors were already approaching her, awaiting her answer on deals that would allow her to turn professional. It would mean she could earn money while competing at an elite level, but she still craved the ordinary experiences her friends were enjoying.

As ever, Ron Junior wasn't afraid to give his opinion.

'Opportunities like this are once in a lifetime,' he said. 'Your next chance will be Tokyo in 2020, and so much can happen between now and then. You'll be 23 and you might not be able to flip, twist and jump the way you do now.'

After weeks spent wrestling with her choices, Simone came to a decision. 'You've got a chance to fulfil your Olympic dream,' she said to herself. 'Take it. College can wait.' Deep down she knew it was the right choice. And as soon as she announced it on Twitter, she was bombarded with messages of support.

Gymnastics was now her job. Her career had officially begun. And with it, the opportunity to fulfil another childhood dream: she signed with GK Elite Sportswear to design her own set of leotards!

To celebrate her decision, she went on holiday to Bora Bora with a couple of close friends.

As she spent the next few weeks relaxing on the

beach and binge-watching old episodes of *Beverly Hills, 90210*, Ron Junior called her: 'Hold on to your holiday spirit, Simone. Enjoy every minute leading up to Rio. Don't think too far ahead.'

These words stayed with Simone as she performed at the Pacific Rim Championships in April 2016. As well as a samba-inspired floor routine that she thought would appeal to Brazilian audiences in Rio, she excelled at the Cheng on vault. With a difficulty score of six, it was a move that most gymnasts avoided. But Simone nailed it, keeping her toes pointed and legs perfectly straight to ensure her execution was flawless.

But it was a different story a few months later at the P&G National Championships. Simone struggled to perform her routines as perfectly as she wanted to. Simone still came away with gold on all-around – her fourth National Championships win – but as her friends and family congratulated her, she didn't feel like celebrating. She knew she hadn't performed to the highest standard she could.

'I want to do better,' she told Aimee.

'You will, Simone.'

And Simone was well aware she couldn't perform her best at Rio without the support, friendship or experience of her teammates. At 22, Aly was a few years older than the other girls and had already won two Olympic gold medals. She kept a firm hand on the team's behaviour too, especially Simone, who was fond of snacking on sweets.

'You've got enough energy – for goodness sake! You'll be all over the place on those beams in practice tomorrow! You'll never sleep, and sleep is important to be at your best.'

'What else?' Simone was keen for any advice she could get. 'How can I be at my best at Rio?'

Aly paused for a moment.

'There's always so much pressure to succeed at the Olympics. Yes, they're a special, once in a lifetime occasion. But you've got to remember they're just another event. Think of them as any other practice. Okay?'

'Okay.'

'Oh, and remember not to look at the Olympic rings!'

CHAPTER 19

THE FINAL FIVE

It was the end of the Olympic trials and Simone, along with four other gymnasts – Gabby Douglas, Aly Raisman, Madison Kocian and Laurie Hernandez – had been chosen to represent their country at Rio. As red, white and blue confetti swirled all around them, Simone felt overcome with joy and happiness at the thought of representing her country. Tears welled up in her eyes as they all hugged each other tight.

'We're going to Rio, girls!'

The iconic sights of Rio – Corcovado, Cristo de Redentor and Copacabana Beach – flashed through her mind. Simone couldn't believe she'd soon see them all for real.

But a week later, she was struggling with her routine on the new bars. They were a different kind and she couldn't get used to how springy they were.

'You've got to get used to them, I'm afraid, Simone, you'll be competing on them in Rio. Let's call it a day for now. I can see you're frustrated,' said Aimee.

When Simone arrived home, she fell on to her bed and began to cry. All her old fears and anxieties had come flooding back and she felt powerless to control them. Her cries turned to sobs and soon she was struggling to catch her breath. She couldn't get the thought of crashing down to the mat from the bars in front of millions of people out of her head.

Her dad appeared at the doorway. 'Honey, what's wrong?'

Simone sobbed even harder now. She finally managed to say: 'Everyone thinks I'm going to win,

Dad. The papers, social media, the whole country... what if I let them all down?'

Her dad pulled her into a hug. 'Sweetheart, you won't let anyone down. I promise you.'

But when Simone's tears wouldn't stop coming, her dad came up with an idea. 'Would talking to Mr Andrews, the sports psychologist, help? I can call him.'

Within 10 minutes, Simone was speaking to Mr Andrews. She felt a wave of relief wash over her as she heard his kind, calming voice.

'I don't think I'm ready,' she told him. 'Everyone expects me to win, but I'm not sure I can.'

'Yes, maybe everyone does expect you to win... But what can you actually control out there?'

Simone answered without thinking. 'Being the best I can be.'

'So, just focus on that. Let everyone have their expectations. You can't change those.'

Simone immediately felt calmer and more in control. The following day, her routines went well during practice. That evening, she and the team began to share ideas for their team name. They thought back to some of the legendary teams who had represented their country before them: 'Magnificent Seven', 'Fierce Five'. How did they want to be remembered?

Finally, Aly said: 'This is the last year there are going to be five competitors in a team. How about "Final Five?"

They all agreed. It was a fitting tribute to Martha, too. She was retiring the following year and they would be the final five gymnasts under her tuition.

Simone felt apprehensive as she and the team travelled to their training camp for ten days before heading to Rio. She would only see her family one more time before she went out to Rio. They were flying out separately. Without thinking, she sat down and wrote a note to them.

'Hi Mom and Dad, I love you all. See you soon in Rio. I will make you proud.'

As she imagined Nellie's face reading it, tears

welled up in her eyes. Ahead of her was the most important competition in her life, and she wanted her family to know how much they meant to her.

***

Ten days of intensive training flew by, and soon the Final Five were on their way to Rio. As the plane touched down, Simone saw blue skies and mountains through the window. Excitement began to bubble in her chest. She was here! This was really happening!

The team gasped in amazement as they took in the sights of the Olympic Village. There was a pool, workout studios and a canteen that was open 24 hours a day, serving cuisine from all over the world. Simone began to salivate as she took in all the pizza on offer.

'And it's all completely free!' she said in amazement. 'I'm so hungry.'

Aly immediately brought them all back down

to earth: 'Such a shame we can't eat it.' Her teammates groaned as she steered them towards healthier options of steamed chicken and fish.

One afternoon as they were eating together in the canteen, a tall, muscular man walked past their table. Aly and Gabby nearly exploded out of their seats with excitement.

They hissed: 'It's Usain Bolt!'

'Let's get his picture!'

But one of the men he was with stopped them in their tracks. 'Let him eat dinner, please.'

Aly said, 'We'd better apologise later.'

After they finished their meal, they walked over to Usain's table.

'You must be the US gymnastics team,' he said, giving them a big smile.

'Is it that obvious?' asked Gabby.

'Kind of.' Usain grinned.

Whereas Usain Bolt was well over six feet tall, the gymnastics team barely measured more than five feet each. Gymnasts are known for being small, but at four feet, eight inches, Simone was the smallest. In fact, she was the shortest of the 555 US Olympic athletes competing in Rio.

In between workouts, the team relaxed on their balcony watching their favourite show, *Modern Family*, or dancing to their favourite song of the tournament: Jake Miller's 'Overnight'. Simone laughed when she caught an interview on the TV with the mums of all the team members.

'Listen to this, guys – apparently they're more nervous than us!' she said.

'I know,' said Gabby. 'Are you nervous?'

Simone shook her head, and so did the rest of the Final Five.

'See, we're confident. No need to be nervous.'

'Girls, we're more than confident,' said Aly, grinning. 'We're invincible!'

***

Within the first few weeks of the games kicking

off, Team USA sailed through the qualifying rounds and into the final. They fought off competition from their old rivals, China and Russia, to win gold with a total all-around score of 185.238. The next morning, Simone awoke to feel the weight of the gold medal in her hand, proof that the day before hadn't all been a dream.

But they knew their task wasn't over yet. They still had the individual all-around competition and event finals to compete in. As the top qualifiers from the team win, Simone and Aly would be representing Team USA in the coveted all-around final. In two days' time, they would be battling it out with competitors from around the globe.

And the whole world would be watching.

CHAPTER 20

A PERFECT LANDING

'It's weird,' Simone told Aly as the girls met for breakfast in the vast village canteen on the morning of the final. 'I'm still not really nervous.'

The smile on her face was so infectious that Aly beamed back at her. 'Me neither.'

'Actually, I'm mostly excited,' said Simone.

'Same!'

Back in their apartment, they took one final look at the leotards they'd laid out the night before. Aly had chosen a shiny red number with lines of crystals fanning out from the neckline, while Simone picked a patriotic leotard inspired by the

American flag with red and white stripes dotted with stars.

As they did each other's hair and make up, Simone felt so excited that she struggled to keep her hand steady.

'Careful!' warned Aly. 'I don't want to look like a clown!'

'Sorry!' giggled Simone.

'Whatever happens today, you're awesome, you know that,' Aly said.

Simone felt a glow of pleasure. She had always looked up to her more experienced teammate. She loved that they were now firm friends.

'*Whatever happens today, you're awesome,*' she repeated, before throwing her arms around her friend.

It was time. As they walked out onto the floor to join the other top contenders from Russia, China and Brazil, the entire crowd was whooping and cheering. Simone's heart went out to the high-spirited audience, but most of all to her mom

Nellie's voice, which she could still hear through the din: 'You've got this, Simone!'

'Just like practice,' she whispered to herself. Then she saluted the judges and took off down the runway for her first event on vault. And what better way to start than with the Amanar!

But there was a little bit too much adrenaline in her body, too much power in her legs. As she soared through the air, she knew she wouldn't stick her landing.

Oops!

But the tumbles and twists had been impressive. Even with the final hop on the mat, the judges still awarded her a score of 15.86. Simone grinned with delight. It was enough to put her in the lead.

With her first event out of the way, Simone's routines flowed seamlessly. On bars, she felt as though she was having an out-of-body experience. From her Tkatchev to her Pak salto and dismount, it was one of the best bar routines she'd ever done. The roar of the crowd as she returned to the mat was ear-splitting.

But it wasn't enough to keep her in first place. Russia's Aliya Mustafina – the master of bars – was ahead.

There were still two events to go, though, and Simone had a good feeling as she hopped up onto the beam. *This is going to go well!*

She was right. Each skill connected smoothly and even the double twisting double tuck – one of the hardest dismounts in the world – felt effortless and easy. As she stuck a perfect landing, the arena erupted. She threw her arms up in the air and lifted her chest proudly. Her performance couldn't have gone better – and the judges agreed. With a score of 15.433, she'd retaken the lead.

As Simone prepared to step onto the mat for floor, Aimee caught her arm. 'Just go and enjoy it,' she told her.

Simone grinned. That wouldn't be hard! She couldn't stop smiling as she leapt through the air to the samba rhythms that she and Aimee had chosen.

The crowd cheered and clapped along as she performed her final tumbling pass. And when her score flashed up on the screen, the arena exploded in a wave of noisy support. 15.933. She'd got the gold!

Simone ran into the arms of Aimee and Aly, before lifting her hands in an ecstatic victory salute to the crowd. As tears of joy and gratitude ran down her face, she knew that she would remember this day forever. Who knew what the future might bring – but whatever happened, nothing could take this magical moment away from her.

***

Simone went on to win gold for vault and floor, as well as bronze on beam, bringing her Olympic medal total to five. Five medals! It hardly seemed real. The days that followed were a whirlwind of press interviews, TV appearances and photo shoots, as everyone clamoured to meet one of the most decorated female athletes at the Olympics. Simone Biles was a record-breaker: the first American gymnast to win four gold medals at a single Games. She was now an icon!

Despite her new fame, Simone was shocked when her agent, Janey Miller, told her the American athletes had voted for her to carry the country's flag at the Olympic closing ceremony. It was the first time an American gymnast had ever been chosen.

She gulped as she pictured herself walking through Maracanã Stadium, with tens of millions across the world watching her.

'That flag is practically the same height as me – what if I drop it?'

'You've got the strength, dedication and skill to win five Olympic medals for your country!' Janey laughed. 'But you're worried you might drop a flag?'

Simone grinned. Okay, maybe it did sound a bit silly. 'But you know what,' she added. 'I'm going to be so dwarfed by that flag... perhaps no one will even notice me!'

There was little chance of that. No one could miss Simone, or the huge smile on her face, as she carried the flag through the arena and past the cheering crowds. She could never have predicted that she, the smallest American athlete at the Games, would be asked to carry a flag twice her size. How far she had come! Her feeling of pride as she stared around her was accompanied by a huge sense of peace. She had done it. She had overcome every obstacle to achieve her dream.

Afterwards, another surprise... President Barack Obama and First Lady Michelle Obama had tweeted her: 'Couldn't be prouder of #TeamUSA. Your determination and passion inspired so many of us. You carried that flag high tonight @Simone_Biles!'

Simone was gobsmacked. A special mention from the US president! It didn't get much bigger than that!

She didn't think it was possible to feel happier

and more excited than she did at that moment. But it turned out it was! Simone, Aly and the rest of Team USA were due to appear on the *Today Show* with the host Hoda Kotb. Hoda had joked to Simone that she'd invited Zac Efron onto the show. Simone had been a huge fan of his, ever since she'd watched him in *High School Musical*.

'Ha! I think I'm gonna need a defibrillator.' Simone had laughed.

Hoda's eyes were twinkling. Moments later, Simone's jaw fell open as Zac strode out onto the set. The rest of the team started screaming, while Simone hid behind Aly, her hands covering her face.

When she finally emerged, she was bright red. Zac swept her up onto his hip and gave her a big kiss on the cheek.

'I can't believe this is happening!' Simone yelped, before dissolving into giggles.

Zac smiled unassumingly. 'When I found out you guys were fans, I had to come and hang out with you. You're America's true heroes right now.'

'Simone Biles is having the most perfect week of her life,' wrote one newspaper article a few days later. Simone had to agree. However, she couldn't wait to see where life would take her after the Olympics. There was always another goal to set or challenge ahead: a life of dreams and possibilities stretched before her.

But for now, with her family and friends around her, she was ready to bask in the joy of what she'd accomplished so far.

CHAPTER 21

LIFE AFTER RIO

With her dance partner, Sasha Farber, beside her, Simone twirled gracefully across the floor to Demi Lovato's 'Skyscraper'. As the music faded, Simone and Sasha took their final pose, before falling into each other's arms and hugging. The TV audience erupted with cheers and whoops. It was 2017 and Simone was taking a year off to explore different pursuits. And for eight weeks, she had wowed the crowds on *Dancing With the Stars*, proving to be just as talented a dancer as she was a gymnast.

'That was brilliant, Simone!' whispered Sasha. 'Well done!'

'Thank you!' grinned Simone. She had loved learning to dance. And in her gold-sequinned outfit, she had never felt so glamorous! She knew how lucky she was to be having this extraordinary experience. It was just one of many new things she had done since taking some time out.

But it wasn't long before Simone yearned to return to the thrill of flipping and flying through the air again. Towards the end of the year, she was back training in her parents' gym with new coaches, Cecile and Laurent Landi. Aimee had moved to Florida to take on a new coaching role. Though Simone knew Aimee would be irreplaceable – she had guided her through so many trials and tribulations – Simone had a new goal: to become world class on uneven bars. And if anyone could help her to achieve this, it was the Landis, who had guided Madison Kocian to silver on bars in Rio.

'It feels good to be back.' She beamed, looking around the familiar gym, a sprawling 56,000 square feet, filled with state-of-the-art equipment.

Her whole body was fizzing with energy, eager to be back doing what she was best at.

After so much time away, it wasn't easy to get back into competitive shape. Before long, she was training six hours a day, six days a week. It was tough, tiring and some days Simone couldn't help wondering what she was doing – did she really want to be pushing her body to its limits again? But her favourite tunes – such as 'Eastside' by benny blanco, Halsey & Khalid – kept her motivated through gruelling training sessions.

And as the weeks went by, she began to feel the improvement on bars that she had hoped for. After successfully adding a new move to her dismount – Shaposh half and double-double – she high-fived Laurent. 'This makes it all worth it,' she said.

He smiled at her. 'You're definitely making progress, Simone.'

***

When it came to competition, Simone had lost none of her competitive spirit. At the US Classic in July 2018, she wowed the crowds with new additions to her routine, including the Fabrichova – a double-twisting double tuck off the bars – to win the all-around title and claim the highest score of any gymnast in the past two years.

It was just the first of many performances over the next two years that would astonish audiences and commentators.

In October 2018 Simone was about to perform her own new vault move in the qualifiers for the World Championships in Doha. Her coaches were concerned, though. The night before, she'd been admitted to hospital with severe stomach pains caused by a kidney stone. But Simone was determined to go ahead with the competition.

'Are you sure you want to do this, Simone?' asked Laurent.

'Yeah, sure. I mean, I'm in pain but the

adrenaline's going to help me nail this.'

Laurent smiled. 'I shouldn't really say this, but sometimes I think you might be a superhero.'

Simone shrugged. 'If I pull this off, I'll call my stone the Doha Pearl.'

Miraculously, she did. Her new move was given such a high D rating that it tied with the Produnova for the most difficult women's vault ever completed.

It instantly became known as 'The Biles'.

With routines that were significantly more difficult than those of her competitors, Simone went on to win gold in all-around and vault at Doha. She had now won a mind-blowing 13 World Championships gold medals, breaking Belarusian Vitaly Scherbo's previous record of 12. And her hard work on the bars had paid off too: she won silver on uneven bars and bronze on beam. Finally, with a gold on floor, she became the first US gymnast to win a medal on every single event at a single World Championships.

Was there anything Simone couldn't do?

***

'Are you sure about this, honey?'

Simone and her mother were picking out leotards for the US National Gymnastics Championships in Missouri, the next major competition after the World Championships. Simone had picked a brand new design: a grey leotard with a picture of a goat on the back (standing for 'greatest of all time') with the surname Biles in sparkly sequins.

'Yes, I'm going to wear it.'

She had been criticised by some people online for wearing a leotard with her surname on the back at the US Classic in July.

She gave Nellie a big hug. 'It's just a little joke. Like a nod to the haters,' she said. 'Don't worry, Mom. I'm always striving to be better, no matter how good I get. So I can't ever be the greatest right?'

But a few months later at the World Championships in Stuttgart, Simone successfully unveiled two more gravity-defying new moves.

Mary Lou Retton, one of the US's most successful ever gymnasts had called her 'the greatest gymnast of all time'. And it was clear few could dispute this now.

The Stuttgart crowds went crazy as Simone executed a perfect triple double – a double backflip with three twists – at the beginning of her floor routine. She went on to perform a double-double dismount off the balance beam. Neither skill had ever been completed on an international stage and it didn't take long for the moves to go viral.

It was also in Stuttgart that Simone won her 24th World Championships medal. She now held the record for most medals won at the World Championships, surpassing Scherbo's previous record.

If Simone's fans were beginning to wonder what feats she might aim to pull off at the Tokyo Olympics, they didn't have to wait long to find out. In February 2020 Simone completed a Yurchenko with a double flip: a move considered to be so dangerous that no female gymnast had ever risked it in competition. When she posted a video of her performance on Twitter, fans around the world went crazy. But there was one special fan whose approval meant the world to Simone.

'Wow, Simone! Just incredible!' said Aimee, on the phone from Florida. 'You're unstoppable. You put your heart and soul into every move, and you just keep on pushing the boundaries of what's possible.'

Simone smiled. 'Well, as long as I've got passion and determination, I'm just going to keep on going,' she said proudly. 'For as long as my body will let me.'

Olympic Medals

- Rio 2016: Individual All-Around, Gold;
  Floor Exercise, Gold; Horse Vault, Gold;
  Balance Beam, Bronze; Team All-Around, Gold

World Championship Medals

- Antwerp 2013: All-Around, Gold;
  Floor Exercise, Gold; Vault, Silver;
  Balance Beam, Bronze
- Nanning 2014: Team, Gold;
  All-Around, Gold; Balance Beam, Gold;
  Floor Exercise, Gold; Vault, Silver
- Glasgow 2015: Team, Gold;
  All Around, Gold; Balance Beam, Gold;
  Floor Exercise, Gold; Vault, Bronze
- Doha 2018: Team, Gold; All-Around, Gold;
  Vault, Gold; Floor Exercise, Gold;
  Uneven Bars, Silver, Balance Beam, Bronze
- Stuttgard 2019: Team, Gold;
  All-Around, Gold; Vault, Gold;
  Floor Exercise, Gold; Balance Beam, Gold

NAME:	Simone Biles
DATE OF BIRTH:	**14 March 1997**
PLACE OF BIRTH:	Columbus, Ohio, USA
NATIONALITY:	**American**
SPORT:	Artistic Gymnastics
Height:	**143 cm**
Main events:	Team, Floor Exercise, Balance Beam, Vault, All-Around
Club:	**World Champions Centre**
Coach:	Laurent Landi and Cecile Canqueteau-Landi

Olympic Medals

GOLD 

SILVER 

BRONZE 

World Championship Medals

GOLD 

SILVER 

BRONZE